A Miracle at (

GW01466046

How One Act of Kindness Reve

By Bianca Vad

A Miracle at Christmas

This is a work of fiction. Names, characters, places, and incidents are either products of the author's imagination or used fictitiously. Any resemblance to actual events, locales, or persons, living or dead, is purely coincidental.

Scripture quotations, where used, are taken from the **Holy Bible, New International Version (NIV)** unless otherwise noted.

Cover Design by Bianca Vadivellu

Editing & Interior Layout by Bianca Vadivellu

Published by Bianca Vadivellu

Prologue: The Prayer She Stopped Praying

The air in the sterile, harshly lit hospital waiting room was a suffocating blend of antiseptic and suppressed grief. Outside, the early spring storm battered the windows, a cruel, indifferent echo to the tempest raging inside **Grace Lawson**. The digital clock on the wall, an unfeeling arbiter of time, declared it 2:14 AM. It was two hours since the police had delivered the news—a sudden, brutal car accident on a slick patch of highway.

Grace sat gripping the leather-bound Bible **Tom** had given her on their first anniversary, its pages worn smooth from years of shared devotion. She was thirty-three then, her faith an unshakeable fortress, a deep, warm reservoir she had drawn from since childhood. Tom was her anchor, his booming laughter and steadfast kindness the living proof of God's grace in her life. Now, he was behind those double doors, a life suspended by the relentless, rhythmic *beep-beep-beep* of the monitors—a sound that was either the whisper of hope or the prelude to silence.

She had always believed in the power of prayer. Her mother had taught her that God was near, that He heard every plea, great or small. But as the minutes stretched into an eternity, Grace felt that certainty dissolving, melting away under the intense, crushing pressure of reality. This was not a misplaced car key or a tough job interview; this was the foundational beam of her life threatening to give way. This required a miracle.

She lifted the Bible, tears blurring the gilt edges of the pages. Her head bowed over the familiar script, she began to pray—not the polite, measured prayers of the Sunday service, but a raw, desperate howl of the soul.

"Please, Father, I know You are sovereign. I know You have a plan. But his purpose here isn't finished. You know how much good he does; You know how many people he helps. Please, Lord, give him back to me. Mend what is broken. Let Your perfect will be for healing, for restoration. Don't take him, please. Not yet. I cannot do this without him. I can't. Please, I am begging you. Let there be a miracle."

She prayed until her voice was a hoarse whisper and her throat ached with the effort. She prayed for so long that the leather imprint of the cross on the Bible cover was pressed into her cheek. She emptied herself of every plea, every verse, every ounce of conviction she possessed, laying it all out before the Almighty, awaiting the immediate, undeniable presence of divine intervention. She expected the doors to open, the doctor's face to be wreathed in surprise and joy, proclaiming the impossible reversal of fate.

But the only thing that followed was the cold, indifferent **silence** of the waiting room.

The hospital doors eventually swung open, but not for the miracle. A kind, tired-looking doctor stepped out, his face grave, his voice gentle as he delivered the words that sliced through Grace's reality like broken glass. The words were clinical, final, and utterly devastating. Tom was gone. The prayers had not been answered. The miracle had not arrived.

In that frozen moment, Grace felt not just grief, but a profound, shocking **betrayal**. If God was loving, if He was listening, if He was truly powerful, why the silence? Why the denial? She had given Him everything—her faith, her devotion, her final, desperate plea—and He had given her back nothing but an empty space and the crushing weight of sorrow.

Later, when she was finally alone in the silence of their home, the scent of Tom's unused shaving cream still lingering in the air, Grace walked slowly to the bookshelf. She picked up the Bible, not with reverence, but with a weary, defeated finality. She placed it back on the shelf, wedging it tightly between volumes of poetry and local history, where it would remain untouched.

That night, she knelt by the bed, the familiar place of their evening prayers. But she didn't pray. She stared into the darkness, the silence of the room mirroring the silence she had received from above.

She made a quiet, definitive vow to the empty space where her faith had once resided: **She would never pray again.**

Five years later, the Bible remained untouched, a silent testament to the grief that had not just taken her husband, but had also extinguished the light of her belief. Her kindness remained, a gentle echo of Tom's nature, but her conversation with Heaven was definitively closed.

Chapter 1: Winter in Evergreen Valley

Evergreen Valley lived up to its name, particularly in the days leading up to Christmas. The small, mountain-ringed town was already blanketed in a perfect, crystalline layer of snow, and every street corner, every lamppost, and every storefront was draped in a breathtaking tapestry of festive lights. The air smelled crisp, clean, and faintly of woodsmoke and peppermint—the quintessential scent of a **Currier & Ives Christmas card**.

For anyone visiting, the atmosphere was intoxicating, a tangible sense of magic and anticipation. But for **Grace Lawson**, the owner of *Bloom & Believe*, a small flower shop nestled just off Main Street, the festive splendor felt like a dazzling, painful spotlight on her own internal gloom.

She was thirty-eight now, her face still possessing the quiet beauty that Tom had loved, but her eyes held a weariness that had settled there five years ago and refused to leave. She was methodical in her work, transforming her little shop into a sanctuary of holiday greenery. The scent of fresh-cut pine, cyclamen, and white lilies filled the air, a scent she found calming in its predictability. She worked quickly, her hands adept at weaving ribbons and setting perfect bows, ensuring her shop was visually flawless for the onslaught of last-minute Christmas shoppers.

Yet, as she hung the single, unlit wreath on her front door—a silent protest against the brilliant display all around her—she felt utterly

disconnected. The lights were beautiful, but they couldn't penetrate the cool, polished wall she had built around her heart. Christmas was merely a season of high volume for her business, a necessary hurdle to be cleared before the quiet hibernation of January.

The small bell above the door chimed, announcing a visitor. **Pastor Daniel Hayes** entered, bringing with him a gust of cold air and a sense of warm, robust goodwill. Daniel was forty-two, tall, with kind eyes and a persistent, gentle nature. He had been a close friend of Tom's and had shepherded Grace through the initial, devastating waves of grief.

"Grace, this shop is a masterpiece, as always," Daniel greeted her, stamping the snow from his polished leather shoes. He picked up a pot of vibrant red poinsettias. "You bring more beauty to Evergreen Valley than the lights themselves."

"Thank you, Pastor," Grace replied, managing a polite, professional smile that didn't quite reach her eyes. She retreated behind her counter, arranging small cellophane packets of flower food. "But I just sell the beauty; I don't create it."

Daniel recognized the subtle distancing, a reflex he had encountered countless times over the last five years. He placed the poinsettias back down and leaned an elbow on the counter.

"It's Christmas Eve service tomorrow night, Grace," he reminded her gently, his tone conversational, not demanding. "It's Communion. The candlelight service. Your favorite hymn, 'Silent Night,' is the closing piece. It would mean the world to the congregation, and to me, to see you there."

Daniel never pushed aggressively, knowing that Grace's resistance was rooted in deep pain, not stubbornness. He simply extended the invitation, believing that God's persistent love would eventually find the right moment to break through.

Grace kept her eyes focused on the flower food. "That's very kind, Daniel. But I'm afraid I'm swamped. Christmas Eve is one of our busiest times for emergency arrangements and last-minute pickups. I simply can't spare the time."

She knew it was a thinly veiled excuse. Her shop would close at 3:00 PM on Christmas Eve. But the thought of sitting in the familiar wooden pew, surrounded by the joyful reverence of the season, and having to sing a hymn that spoke of **holy peace** when her own heart felt nothing but sterile emptiness, was unbearable. It felt like hypocrisy. She had stopped attending church shortly after Tom's death, unable to reconcile the unwavering faith preached there with the unanswered prayer she carried like a heavy stone.

"Grace, you are always welcome. No need to explain," Daniel assured her, his tone warm. He paid for a small bouquet of white roses—a weekly purchase for his own mantel—and walked toward the door. "Just know that the light is still on for you, inside and outside the church."

He left, and the bell chimed once more, leaving Grace alone with the scent of lilies and the pervasive, manufactured glow of the holiday.

A few minutes later, needing to move, Grace bundled up in her heavy woolen coat and stepped outside to brush the fresh snow off the pots of spruce that lined her walkway. The scene was picture-perfect: families laughing, children dragging new sleds, and the continuous soft melody of Christmas carols piped through the town speakers.

Then, her gaze fell upon a young woman and two small children struggling near the bus stop across the street.

The woman, who looked to be in her late twenties, was clearly exhausted. She was bundled in a thin, worn coat, clutching a collapsing plastic grocery bag that held a sad, meager collection of supplies. Her two children clung to her—a girl, perhaps eight, with bright, anxious eyes, and a small boy, maybe five, whose face was pink and runny from the cold.

The scene wasn't dramatic; it was just a quiet portrait of ordinary **struggle**. The woman—**Sarah Miller**, though Grace didn't know her name—looked tired, not defeated, but fighting a losing battle against the cold and the weight of her responsibilities. The little boy slipped on a patch of ice, causing Sarah to instinctively shift the grocery bag to catch him. The bag split entirely, scattering a small carton of milk, a loaf of bread, and a few canned goods into the grimy slush near the curb.

Sarah sank onto her knees, not from injury, but from sheer, hopeless fatigue, trying desperately to salvage the ruined groceries while shielding the children from the traffic. The little girl, Lily, started to cry softly, her small hands unable to grasp the wet, cold items.

Grace watched from across the street. Her logical mind, the part she relied on, argued that this was not her problem. This was the burden of the social services, the responsibility of the community outreach program that she no longer participated in.

But her **heart**, the old, deeply empathetic heart that Tom had loved, **ached**. It was a physical sensation, a sudden, sharp pang of familiar, compassionate pain. It was a sensation she hadn't allowed herself to feel fully in five years, the kind of selfless, immediate need to help that Tom had always embodied.

She looked at the children, their faces etched with the cold and the shared worry of their mother's burden. She saw not strangers, but a simple, vulnerable family in immediate, undeniable need. The cold logic of her grief momentarily gave way to the enduring, instinctive kindness she couldn't fully extinguish.

Grace threw caution to the wind. She crossed the street, stepping over the glistening, immaculate snow of the crosswalk and into the messy, complicated reality of Sarah Miller's life.

Chapter 2: A Chance Encounter

The transition from the pristine, manufactured beauty of Evergreen Valley's Main Street to the raw, messy reality of human struggle was abrupt, almost jarring. **Grace Lawson** crossed the street, stepping quickly over the crosswalk and into the slushy gutter where the remnants of the fallen groceries lay scattered. The cold, wet reality of the situation immediately replaced the sterile professionalism she maintained in her shop.

The young mother, **Sarah Miller**, was still crouched in the snow, her slender shoulders hunched in exhaustion and humiliation, trying to scoop up the ruined carton of milk with frozen fingers. The little girl, **Lily**, stood rigidly beside her, her eyes wide with fear, and the boy, **Ben**, had buried his face into his mother's thin coat, muffled sobs shaking his small frame.

"It's alright, sweetheart," Grace said, her voice surprisingly steady and warm, instantly adopting the tone of calm authority that had always melted away the stress of a hectic day at *Bloom & Believe*. "It's just milk. It's spilled milk. But we can't salvage the bread, I'm afraid."

Sarah looked up, her face etched with a desperate shame that was far more painful to witness than the poverty itself. Her dark hair was escaping its braid, and her cheeks were wind-chapped and red.

"I'm so sorry," Sarah whispered, her voice husky. "I should have held the bag better. It's just been... a long day."

Grace knelt beside her without a moment of hesitation, pulling off the thick, water-resistant gloves she wore for pruning. The cold immediately bit into her skin, a physical reminder of the harsh elements this family was enduring.

"Don't apologize for gravity or bad plastic," Grace insisted gently, collecting the remaining canned goods and placing them carefully into her own large, sturdy canvas tote bag she carried for errands. "The priority now is getting you and the children warm. You can't wait for a bus in this condition."

Sarah immediately began to protest, fueled by a pride that was clearly the last defense she had against asking for help. "Oh, no, we're fine, really. The bus is due any minute. We don't want to bother you, ma'am."

Grace stood up, holding the half-full tote bag. She looked directly at Sarah, meeting her anxious gaze with a quiet firmness that brooked no argument. This was the same look she used when negotiating bulk orders with wholesalers; it was efficient, decisive, and entirely secular. She was not acting on faith; she was acting on logistics and basic **human decency**. This was merely an urgent problem that required immediate, practical intervention.

"The next bus is twenty minutes late, according to the town app, and your son's nose is running. Furthermore, all the food you managed to buy is either ruined or freezing," Grace stated, folding the ruined plastic bag neatly and tucking it into a trash receptacle. "I have a car parked just down the street. It has excellent heating, and I can have you home in less than ten minutes. It is not a bother, Sarah. It is simply the practical solution. Now, let's go."

The firmness in Grace's tone—the refusal to treat this as an awkward charitable exchange—seemed to break through Sarah's wall of protest. Sarah nodded once, a quick, almost defeated dip of her head. Lily instantly looked less anxious, taking Grace's free hand with a trusting, immediate warmth that shocked Grace's own guarded system.

Grace ushered them into her clean, heated sedan, settling the children securely into the back seat. Lily, the eight-year-old, was quiet but observant, immediately focusing on the intricate floral scent that clung to Grace's coat. Ben, the younger one, had already burrowed into the thick wool of his mother's coat, the residual shock making him sleepy.

As Grace drove, she tried to maintain the quiet, non-intrusive silence she had established. But Sarah, relieved and exhausted, felt the need to fill the silence with an explanation—the self-justification of a good person who had fallen on hard times.

"Thank you, ma'am. My name is Sarah Miller, and I really appreciate this," Sarah began, twisting her chapped hands in her lap. "I just lost my cleaning job at the old mill. They shut down for the holidays earlier than expected, and the final check won't clear until after Christmas. I was just trying to get us through the next few days. I'm usually so careful with the bags."

"Please, call me Grace," she replied, keeping her eyes focused on the snowy road. "And please, stop explaining. It's Christmas. People help each other. It's a very old tradition."

But even as she said the words, Grace's mind provided an internal corrective: *This isn't tradition, and it certainly isn't religion. This is simple, practical kindness. This is what Tom would have done. I am doing this for Tom's memory, to keep the good, simple logic of his heart alive, not because of some divine call.*

The drive took them away from the brilliantly lit center of Evergreen Valley and toward a less affluent area on the outskirts of town, known locally as **The Mews**—a collection of older, cheaply constructed rental units tucked behind the main industrial park. The contrast was stark. The town center glowed with thousands of imported LED lights; The Mews was poorly lit, the snow on the narrow sidewalks dirty, and the buildings themselves showed clear signs of neglect: chipped paint, sagging gutters, and cracked windowpanes taped together against the winter wind. The cold here felt harsher, sharper, carrying with it the metallic tang of urban grime rather than the clean scent of pine.

Sarah directed Grace to the back entrance of a poorly maintained duplex. The single external bulb above the shared porch flickered with a weary inefficiency.

"We're here," Sarah said, her voice dropping slightly, the earlier pride returning as a reflexive defense against exposure.

The Aching Silence

Grace parked the car and insisted on carrying the meager bag of groceries, following Sarah and the children up the dark, uneven steps. The inside air of the tiny, ground-floor apartment immediately hit Grace with a physical chill that went beyond the external temperature. It was the heavy, damp cold of a place that was *never* truly warm, a cold that seeped into walls and clothing.

The apartment was painfully small, consisting of a single living area that doubled as the children's bedroom, a tiny, dark kitchen, and a minuscule, drafty bathroom. Everything was clean—Sarah clearly fought hard against the neglect of the building—but everything was also threadbare. The furniture was minimal and chipped, the blankets piled high on the small sofa bed were thin, and the windows, draped with limp, stained curtains, seemed to actively invite the cold inside.

The most shocking realization came when Grace saw the source of their heating—or lack thereof. An old, oil-filled space heater was plugged into the wall, but it was conspicuously **off**.

"I'll get the heat going," Sarah said quickly, moving to switch the unit on. "We usually keep it off until after dinner; trying to conserve."

Grace's breath caught in her throat. Conserving meant they were sacrificing warmth to stretch their limited funds. The thought of Lily and Ben spending the whole day in this biting cold, the temperature barely above freezing indoors, sent a wave of icy panic through Grace. It was the first time in five years that she had been forced to confront a reality that was genuinely, physically painful—a reality she couldn't simply solve with a checkbook or avoid with a detour.

"Sarah, the children," Grace began, her voice strained. "They shouldn't be in this cold. It's well below fifty degrees in here."

"Oh, they're tough," Sarah insisted, pulling a thin sweater more tightly around Lily's shoulders. "They're used to it. We manage. We wear layers, and they know to jump around if they get too cold."

The forced lightness in Sarah's voice, the sheer determination to maintain a facade of control and competence, was heartbreaking. Grace knew Sarah was trying to protect herself from the pity she clearly felt she didn't deserve.

Grace placed the groceries on the counter, immediately looking for the coffee maker. "Well, let's get some hot chocolate in them, then," she said, her hands moving instinctively toward the practical tasks of comfort. She knew better than to offer money or pity; she needed to offer **presence** and **utility**.

While the water heated, Lily pulled a tattered, well-loved picture book from a shelf—a Christmas story about a lost star. She handed it shyly to Grace.

"Will you read it to us?" Lily asked, her bright eyes fixed on Grace.

Grace hadn't read a children's book in years, not since Tom would read to his little niece every Christmas. But seeing the hopeful, expectant face of the child, she couldn't refuse. She settled onto the cold, worn sofa, pulling both children close. Lily leaned into her side with a surprising weight of trust, and Ben, still sniffing, rested his head on Grace's lap.

As Grace read the simple story of faith and finding the way home, the gentle weight of the children, their small, cold bodies seeking warmth and comfort, melted something tightly held within her chest. It was a purely human connection, a profound moment of shared vulnerability that transcended the financial gap between them. For the first time since that terrible night five years ago, Grace felt the intense, specific pain of **longing**—a longing not for Tom, but for the uncomplicated joy of shared love and purpose.

When the cocoa was ready, Grace made sure the children drank every drop. She stayed for another twenty minutes, using her time efficiently. She looked over the refrigerator, noting the sparse contents, and mentally cataloged the lack of winter essentials—no hats, no scarves, and the heater was clearly broken, not just being conserved.

Finally, she rose to leave. Sarah, tears gathering in her eyes, thanked her again, the gratitude overwhelming the protective pride.

"You truly have the heart of an angel, Grace," Sarah whispered. "I don't know how I would have gotten them home, let alone fed them."

Grace simply offered a brief, impersonal handshake and a reassuring smile. "It was nothing, Sarah. Just a neighbor helping out a neighbor. I'll see you around."

She left the freezing apartment, pulling the heavy, dark door shut behind her, plunging the family back into their challenging reality. She walked quickly to her car, the contrast between the apartment's damp chill and the car's heated interior striking her hard.

Neighborly kindness, she insisted to herself, pulling away from The Mews and back toward the twinkling, perfect streets of Evergreen Valley. *Just a good, simple, human transaction. Nothing more complicated than that.*

The Nudge and the Resistance

Grace returned to her home—a beautiful, historic craftsman house behind her flower shop, meticulously maintained, warm, and smelling faintly of cinnamon and pine potpourri. It was a space that radiated **controlled perfection**. She had ensured the house reflected her current spiritual state: clean, orderly, and entirely devoid of spontaneous emotion or lingering questions.

She made a cup of herbal tea, but the warmth did nothing to chase away the deep, pervasive chill she had absorbed in Sarah's apartment. She tried to read a book, but the words blurred, overshadowed by the stark image of Lily's anxious eyes and the cold, unyielding reality of the broken space heater.

As the evening wore on, the town's Christmas lights outside cast soft, dancing colors on the immaculate walls of her living room. The external cheer of Evergreen Valley pressed in, but now, the festive glow seemed less a mockery and more a **challenge**.

Grace finally gave up the pretense of relaxation and stood by the window, staring out at the silent, snow-covered landscape. And then, she felt it.

It wasn't a voice. It wasn't a vision. It was a deep, undeniable, and intensely unwelcome **pressure** in the center of her chest, right behind her ribs—a sensation that felt like an internal vibration, a gentle, insistent **nudge** that disturbed the polished tranquility of her soul.

The nudge was a memory, too. It felt like the warm, familiar conviction she had carried during her years of devotion, the unshakeable certainty that she was not alone, that her actions had meaning beyond the immediate physical consequence.

You can't just stop there, Grace. You saw the need. The practical help isn't enough.

She recognized the source immediately. It was the echo of the **Divine Providence** she had spent five years carefully walling herself off from. It was the reminder that her hands, adept at weaving ribbons and arranging lilies, were capable of *more* than just commerce—they were capable of being instruments of grace.

The resistance she felt was immediate, visceral, and fierce. It was the resurrection of the grief and the betrayal she had buried when Tom died. She spoke aloud into the empty room, her voice harsh and brittle.

"No," she whispered, shaking her head sharply. "You do not get to claim this. You were silent when I begged you for a miracle. You left me with nothing but loss and the knowledge that my most faithful prayers were ignored."

She began to pace the room, the arguments building into a silent, internal scream.

*I helped Sarah because of Tom! Because his memory dictates that human beings should not be cold and hungry on Christmas. This is secular compassion. This is guilt management. This is anything but **faith**.*

The nudge intensified, a quiet, profound counter-argument in the stillness of her spirit. *The source of the compassion doesn't matter, Grace. The need is real. The action is yours. Your broken heart is still capable of love, and that love is calling you to move.*

Grace resisted with all the analytical, logical strength she possessed. She had established a perfect, protected perimeter around her grief. To answer this call—to continue helping Sarah beyond the simple ride and the hot chocolate—would mean cracking that perimeter. It would mean allowing **purpose** back into her life, and purpose inevitably led to **vulnerability**, which inevitably led to **pain** if that purpose was taken away again.

If she truly gave herself over to helping Sarah, and that help failed, or Sarah let her down, or something went wrong, the emotional damage would be profound. It was safer, cleaner, and less painful to remain disconnected.

She spent the entirety of the night in this spiritual deadlock. She tried to force herself to sleep, but the image of Ben's tear-stained face and the memory of the freezing air in the apartment were too vivid. Every time she closed her eyes, the gentle, insistent **nudge** returned, a quiet, relentless invitation to step outside the safe walls of her grief and engage with the world's unpredictable, messy needs.

As the first faint light of dawn broke over Evergreen Valley, painting the snow-covered mountains in shades of rose and grey, Grace was still awake. She was exhausted, emotionally drained, but ultimately, she had held the line. She had not prayed. She had not committed to any further action. She was determined that her involvement with

Sarah Miller would remain a single, isolated act of **practical human kindness** and nothing more.

But even in her defiance, a small, terrifying seed of realization had been planted: *She knew where Sarah lived, she knew the extent of the need, and she had the means to alleviate it.* The knowledge itself felt like a heavy burden, a responsibility she could not simply return to the shelf like her leather-bound Bible.

The day had begun, and with it, the undeniable fact that her heart, though wounded, had been **stirred**.

Chapter 3: A Heart Stirred

The morning after her sleepless night, **Grace Lawson** felt the lingering exhaustion of a spiritual battle fought to a draw. She hadn't surrendered to the "nudge" of divine conscience, but she hadn't achieved peace in her resistance either. The memory of Sarah's freezing apartment and the sheer vulnerability of the children had lodged itself firmly beneath the cold, clean armor of her grief.

She stood in her own impeccably organized kitchen, the warmth radiating from the vintage gas stove mocking the image of Sarah and her children huddled together. Grace tried to prepare for the day's work at *Bloom & Believe*, but her hands, usually so steady with delicate blossoms, felt clumsy and disconnected. She kept replaying the image of five-year-old Ben's chapped, cold cheek resting against her hand.

"It's not faith," Grace muttered to the empty room, her voice firm, rationalizing the decision she knew she was about to make. "It is **guilt management**. It is simple, logical obligation. I saw a need I can easily alleviate, and as a functioning adult in this community, I have a duty to ensure no children freeze on my watch, regardless of my personal theological disagreements."

The reasoning was sound, clean, and entirely secular. It was a commitment to **human honor**, not to God's plan. By framing it as a logistical necessity and an act of civic responsibility, she could perform the kindness without acknowledging the divine call that scared her. This was not a prayer being answered; this was a problem being solved.

She immediately dressed in her warmest clothes and slipped out of the back door before her first shop employee arrived. She drove straight to the largest grocery store on the edge of Evergreen Valley, choosing a location far from the familiar aisles of the downtown market where she might run into Pastor Daniel or Mrs. Reed. She moved through the aisles with cold, efficient focus, making purchases that were designed for survival and comfort, not mere sustenance.

She bought substantial, durable goods: bags of rice, dried beans, shelf-stable milk, and several packages of dense, nourishing whole-wheat bread. But then, the **human element** broke through her clinical purchasing list. Her hand reached, without conscious permission, for a large canister of gourmet hot cocoa mix—the rich, dark chocolate kind Tom had always insisted on—and a massive bag of brightly colored miniature marshmallows. She also grabbed a beautiful, soft flannel blanket patterned with reindeer and stars, knowing those threadbare layers in Sarah's apartment were insufficient.

The cost was substantial, far beyond the initial partial rent payment she had made the day before (an expense she had quickly categorized as a business deduction). As she stood waiting for the cashier, Grace realized she wasn't just buying food; she was buying **warmth** and **joy**, necessities she had denied herself for five years.

"Are you preparing for a small army, Grace?" the cashier joked, ringing up the heavy, full cart.

Grace managed a thin smile. "Just stocking up for the season," she replied, offering no other explanation, determined to keep this act entirely secret. This was a private transaction between her and her own restless conscience.

The Chill and the Light

When Grace arrived back at The Mews, the apartment complex looked even bleaker than it had the day before, huddled under the morning's fresh layer of snow. The flickering porch light was still struggling against the early winter gloom.

She knocked sharply, balancing the heavy grocery bag and the rolled flannel blanket.

Sarah opened the door, her face a mixture of surprise and profound mortification. She immediately saw the bulk of the bag and the blanket.

"Grace, please, you shouldn't have," Sarah protested, trying to block the doorway instinctively, fueled by that exhausting, powerful pride. "I was going to come down to your shop later and thank you properly for the ride yesterday. We really are fine now."

"You are not fine, Sarah," Grace stated simply, her voice quiet but firm, leveraging the sheer weight of the bag to gain entrance. "And frankly, neither am I. I had a difficult night because I kept thinking about your children being cold. This is as much for my peace of mind as it is for your comfort. Please allow me this selfish act of charity."

The use of the word **selfish**—a pragmatic, self-deprecating motive—seemed to disarm Sarah instantly. Sarah stepped back, her defenses lowering, allowing Grace into the tiny, still-chilly apartment.

Lily and Ben were sitting huddled under a single blanket on the couch, watching a scratched DVD of an old animated Christmas movie. Their eyes widened instantly when they saw Grace, not because of the groceries, but because of the memory of the shared story and the comfort they'd found the day before.

"Auntie Grace!" Ben exclaimed, his voice ringing out with an uninhibited joy that startled Grace. He scrambled off the couch and ran to her, wrapping his small, cold arms around her waist.

The familiar use of an honorific, the instantaneous assumption of closeness and trust, hit Grace with the force of an emotional freight train. It wasn't the distant "ma'am" or "miss," but "Auntie"—a title of family, of belonging, of effortless love. Grace stood frozen for a moment, the heavy grocery bag suddenly feeling weightless, as she felt the full, unfiltered impact of the child's affection.

"Oh, Ben," Grace murmured, kneeling down to meet his gaze. "It's just Grace, sweetheart. I brought more hot chocolate and some new provisions."

Lily, more reserved, walked up and pointed shyly at the flannel blanket. "Is that... for us?"

"It is," Grace confirmed, pulling it free from the bag and shaking out the soft material. The reindeer and stars seemed to wink in the dim light of the apartment. "It's very thick, and it's meant to keep you and Ben warm when you're watching your movies."

Lily gasped—a pure, theatrical sound of eight-year-old delight—and immediately buried herself under the blanket, pulling Ben down with her. The simple, unadulterated pleasure they took in a basic necessity was a deeper emotional blow to Grace than the sight of their poverty. Their joy was an infectious, radiant thing, a tiny, defiant sun in the center of their cold little world.

As Sarah helped Grace unpack the food—her silence now one of grateful awe rather than shame—Grace walked over to the sofa. She sat down, letting the two children nestle against her, sharing the warmth of the new blanket.

"You're too good to us, Grace," Sarah finally managed, her voice thick. "I don't know why you're doing this, but I promise, as soon as I find a new job, I will pay you back every single cent."

"I'm doing this because I can, Sarah," Grace insisted, maintaining her secular distance. "And there is nothing to pay back. We are simply helping each other manage the winter season."

But even as she spoke the words, she knew they were a lie. Her real reason was sitting right beside her, humming softly as she traced the outline of a printed star on the flannel. The children's simple, immediate happiness was a spiritual nourishment Grace hadn't realized she was starving for.

Echoes of Tom's Kindness

It was the sight of Ben trying to lift the heavy can of cocoa mix, his small muscles straining with determined effort, that triggered the **flashback**. The memory flooded Grace's mind with the unexpected warmth and clarity of a summer day.

(Flashback: Five Years Ago, Evergreen Valley Community Hall)

Tom was magnificent when he was helping. It wasn't just the physical strength of the thirty-five-year-old man, a strength honed by a lifetime of carpentry and working outdoors, but the sheer, buoyant joy he took in service.

It was the annual church Christmas food drive, and they were loading heavy boxes of canned goods and frozen turkeys for distribution. Grace, struggling with a particularly unwieldy box of rice, watched Tom effortlessly lift two cartons of milk and a crate of canned soup at once, his face red from exertion and laughter.

"You're going to throw your back out, Tom," she'd warned, tightening the scarf around his neck.

*He hadn't stopped moving, just winked at her over the stack of boxes. "Nonsense, Grace. This is the **best kind of pain**. It's the pain of purpose. Besides, look at this. This isn't a box of food, my darling. This is three weeks of worry we're taking off Mrs. Gable's shoulders. That's a miracle in a cardboard box, and miracles require heavy lifting."*

*He had paused then, catching her gaze, his blue eyes full of genuine, uncomplicated love for his faith and his community. "The best gifts aren't wrapped in paper, Grace. They're wrapped in **action**."*

The flashback snapped Grace back to the cold reality of the apartment, her heart hammering painfully against her ribs. She looked at Ben, struggling with the cocoa can, and the memory of Tom's booming laugh seemed to echo in the tiny room.

Tom had never seen service as a duty; he had seen it as an **expression of joy**. He had never needed a sermon or a divine sign; he had simply seen the need and responded with immediate, full-bodied action, labeling the outcome a "miracle."

A second memory, gentler this time, followed the first. It centered around Tom's philosophy of Christmas giving.

(Flashback: Four Years Ago, The Cozy Quill Bookshop)

Tom had found Grace meticulously wrapping a small, expensive gift for her estranged sister. Grace was focused on the symmetry of the ribbon and the perfect fold of the paper, trying to make the gift speak volumes.

*Tom leaned over her, gently correcting her technique. "You know, you focus so much on the perfect wrapping, you forget the point of the gift," he'd teased, taking the ribbon from her hand. "The wrapping is just the disguise. The real magic is the love the gift represents. And if that love is sincere, it can look messy, be late, or not even be wrapped at all. It just has to be **true**."*

He'd then pulled out a small, roughly carved wooden ornament he had made—a simple star. "This star isn't worth anything, but I made it with true intention. It represents hope. And that," he'd said, pressing it into her hand, "is the most valuable thing you can give someone at Christmas."

Tears suddenly stung Grace's eyes, a rare, uncontrolled outpouring of emotion. She quickly turned her head away so Sarah wouldn't see. The flood of Tom's presence in this cold, impoverished room was overwhelming. His essence wasn't in the church pews she avoided; it was right here, in the practical, humble act of sharing warmth with the cold and vulnerable.

This wasn't about God's silence. This was about **her own silence**—the years she had spent refusing to engage with the kind of immediate, active love that Tom had celebrated, fearing that renewed purpose would only invite renewed pain.

Lily and Ben were the "miracle in the cardboard box" Tom used to speak of, a chance to restore the joy he had shown her, even if she couldn't yet acknowledge the divine source of that joy.

The Compromise of Honor

Grace spent the next hour working with Sarah, helping her organize the new groceries and find better storage solutions. She noticed that the space heater was indeed sputtering—it wasn't just being conserved, it was failing. She discreetly made a mental note to research safe, efficient replacement options.

As she prepared to leave, the children's faces were flushed with warmth, their eyes shining with cocoa and genuine happiness. The change in atmosphere was dramatic; the cold, damp chill was replaced by a small pocket of *light* and *life*.

"You saved us, Grace," Sarah said again, her voice thick with emotion, but this time, the shame was gone, replaced by a fierce, open gratitude. "I truly believe God sent you here."

Grace immediately stiffened, her walls snapping back into place.

"God had nothing to do with it, Sarah," Grace said, trying to keep her voice light and non-confrontational. "I am a local business owner with excess income. You are a neighbor in need. That is the beginning and the end of the story. You have a tough week ahead, and I have a warm home. I simply followed the ethical contract of community."

She offered Sarah a brisk, final hug, a gesture of emotional distance disguised as warmth.

But as she drove away from The Mews, the heavy bag of guilt lifted from her chest and replaced by the simple, enduring sense of **having done the right thing**, Grace finally found the resolution she had been seeking all night.

She could not yet pray to God, the one who had remained silent. But she could **honor Tom**.

She would dedicate her kindness to the enduring legacy of her husband. She would continue to help Sarah and the children, using Tom's memory as her motivation and shield. This way, she could participate in the active, loving kindness that filled her heart, without ever having to surrender to the faith that had shattered her. She could rebuild her life on a foundation of **human goodness**, rooted firmly in the memory of the man she loved.

This is for you, Tom, she thought, the words a silent, solemn vow in the warmth of her car. *I will bring light where there is darkness, just as you always did. This is my way of keeping your spirit alive.*

It was a brilliant compromise, a perfect blend of logic and emotion. It allowed Grace to move forward, motivated by the purest form of human love, while keeping the painful silence of heaven firmly at bay. But she failed to see the subtle trap she had set for herself: **service motivated by human love is often the first, undeniable step back toward divine faith.**

The true miracle wasn't the food she brought, but the fact that a single, tearful plea five years ago was finally, quietly, beginning to be answered—not with the immediate cure she had demanded, but with the subtle, slow, and **perfect timing** of restoration.

Chapter 4: The Struggle Within

The third week of December settled over Evergreen Valley, deepening the snowdrifts and intensifying the festive chaos. For **Grace Lawson**, this chaos was doubled. Externally, *Bloom & Believe* was thriving, the volume of holiday orders demanding her total focus. But internally, Grace was consumed by a meticulous, anxious double life centered entirely around **Sarah Miller** and her children.

Since her pivotal compromise—to help Sarah exclusively in **honor of Tom's memory**—Grace had become a stealth provider. Every morning before the town fully awoke, she would drive to The Mews, dropping off groceries, a tank for the old, sputtering space heater, or vital supplies like thick thermal socks and winter hats. She never stayed long, maintaining a brisk, efficient professionalism that kept the relationship firmly cemented in transactional kindness, not emotional dependence. She had carefully chosen her identity: she was a practical lifeline, not a pastoral friend.

The children, Lily and Ben, continued to dismantle her emotional defenses with their effortless affection, greeting her as "Auntie Grace" and decorating the meager offerings with drawings and handmade paper chains. Their gratitude was a bright, overwhelming light, but it brought with it an uncomfortable shadow: **guilt**.

Grace felt guilty for the disparity between her warm, well-furnished home and Sarah's freezing apartment. She felt guilty for the quiet joy she took in their presence—a joy she hadn't allowed herself to feel since Tom's death. Most profoundly, she felt guilty that she was using her late husband's legacy as a **shield**, performing good deeds out of a human covenant rather than a divine one. She worried that she was mocking the God she no longer trusted by carefully segregating her acts of love.

The mounting pressure finally became unbearable. Grace's meticulous schedule began to fray; she snapped at her otherwise patient assistant and found herself staring blankly at wreaths, unable to summon the decorative focus that had once been second nature. She knew she needed to talk, but she couldn't risk revealing the full truth to Pastor Daniel, who would instantly try to pull her back into the fold of the Church. She needed wisdom, not evangelism.

She decided to seek out **Mrs. Eleanor Reed**.

The Wisdom of Mrs. Reed

Mrs. Reed was a cornerstone of Evergreen Valley's quiet strength. A seventy-year-old widow whose husband had passed after a long, gentle life, Eleanor embodied the kind of **serene, enduring faith** Grace both admired and resented. Eleanor did not preach; she simply *was*. She ran the local volunteer library and served as an unofficial mentor to half the town, offering counsel that was always gentle, deeply Christian, yet grounded in pragmatic, worldly observation.

Grace found her mid-morning, nestled among the stacks of biographies in the warm, dust-scented quiet of the library.

"Eleanor," Grace began, pulling up a chair and lowering her voice. "I need your advice, but I need you to listen to me as a friend, not as Sunday School superintendent. This is about guilt, not God."

Eleanor smiled knowingly, her wise eyes twinkling above her reading spectacles. She placed her book, a collection of C.S. Lewis essays, on the table. "Grace, dear, you can try to compartmentalize your heart, but those two categories rarely stay separate. Go on. Your spirit is troubled, and your flowers are starting to look tense."

Grace laughed, the sound rusty and unfamiliar. She explained everything: the initial chance encounter with Sarah, the shock of the cold apartment, the powerful emotional pull of Lily and Ben, and the internal compromise she had made to keep helping them.

"I only do it because of Tom," Grace insisted, leaning forward, her voice tight with desperation. "He was the one who believed in miracles in cardboard boxes. I'm honoring his light. But the deeper I get, the more this **guilt** piles up. I feel like a fraud. I'm serving others in His name, but I'm doing it from a place of *betrayal*. I'm using human love as a substitute for divine love, and I feel this constant *nudge*, Eleanor, this pressure telling me I'm not doing enough, or that my motives are wrong, or that I'm going to get hurt again."

Eleanor listened patiently, nodding slightly as Grace spoke, tracing the worn spine of her book. When Grace finished, the silence in the library was profound, broken only by the crackle of the gas fireplace.

"You're afraid of the pain of attachment, Grace," Eleanor stated softly. "You believe that if you let God into your purpose, He will let you down again, just as you felt He did when Tom passed. So you keep your actions secular, hiding the source of your compassion behind the lovely, good memory of your husband. And that is a very honorable hiding place."

Grace felt the sting of recognition. "But the guilt, Eleanor. Is it wrong to help only because of Tom?"

Eleanor reached across the table and placed her warm, wrinkled hand over Grace's cold, smooth one. "No, darling. It's never wrong to help. But the pressure you feel isn't guilt over your *motive*; it's **grief over the separation**. You're trying to connect the love in your heart to the love that created it, but you've walled off the path."

She paused, her eyes penetrating Grace's weary gaze. "You ask me if it's wrong to help in Tom's name. Tom was a man of great faith, yes? And every good, loving, selfless action he ever took, where do you think the source of that unending compassion was rooted?"

Grace couldn't speak, knowing the answer was the very thing she was running from.

Eleanor smiled, a deep, knowing warmth spreading across her features. She delivered the line with a gentle, firm conviction that cut straight through Grace's rationalizations.

"God never stopped listening, dear. You just stopped talking."

The words hung in the air, heavy with unspoken truth. Eleanor continued, softening her tone. "Your prayers about Tom felt unanswered because the answer was 'No.' And a 'No' is a devastating answer, my dear, but it is still a form of communication. Silence, true silence, is far crueler. And Grace, you have not received silence. You have received an immediate, direct response to your pain: the moment you allowed yourself to act with Tom's generous spirit, a needy family was placed directly in your path."

"But I prayed for a miracle, Eleanor," Grace whispered, the old pain surfacing, sharp as ever. "I asked for his life back, and I got nothing."

"A miracle is not always the reversal of tragedy, Grace," Eleanor countered, leaning closer. "Sometimes, a miracle is the **renewal of purpose** in the middle of it. And right now, God is using Ben's sticky, cocoa-covered hands to remind you that He hasn't abandoned the conversation. You're talking to Sarah, you're talking to Lily, and you're talking to Tom's memory. It's time you talked to the Source again."

Grace left the library with a pounding heart and a dizzying sense of exposure. Eleanor hadn't given her permission to use Tom as a shield; she had exposed that shield as a paper-thin veil. The conversation had not alleviated the guilt; it had deepened the underlying **spiritual conviction** that her current path, while good, was incomplete.

The Eviction Notice

The weight of this new self-awareness settled heavily over Grace for the next three days, complicating her carefully constructed reality. She increased her offerings to Sarah, bringing a small, portable ceramic heater in place of the sputtering oil-filled one, claiming it was an "inventory surplus."

Then, two days before Christmas Eve, the external crisis Grace had dreaded finally arrived.

She found Sarah sitting on the bottom step of her duplex, huddled in her thin coat, watching Lily and Ben try to draw reindeer in the dirty snow. Sarah's posture was different now; the usual tense resilience was gone, replaced by a devastating, broken despair.

Grace approached cautiously, her gut clenching. "Sarah? What is it? What happened?"

Sarah didn't look up immediately. She simply opened a folded, official-looking document in her lap. It was starkly formal against the drab fabric of her coat: an **Eviction Notice**. The date stamped on the paper demanded the apartment be vacated within forty-eight hours—just after Christmas Day.

"The manager said the partial payment I made last month wasn't enough to cover the fees and late charges that piled up when I lost my previous job," Sarah mumbled, her voice trembling with restrained tears. "They need the full back balance, plus two months' security. And I... I have nothing left, Grace. I got turned down for a cleaning job yesterday. I don't know where to take the children. We'll be sleeping in the old shelter basement by Christmas night."

The devastating finality of the notice hit Grace with physical force. This wasn't a problem she could solve with groceries or hot chocolate. This was a **catastrophe** that threatened to erase the small, fragile foothold Sarah had fought so hard to maintain. This was the moment where secular kindness ran into its limits, where human effort had failed, and where true intervention was required.

Grace felt the familiar surge of panic—the fear of a situation spiraling beyond her control, the echo of the night Tom died. *If I help her with this, I am fully invested. If I fail, the emotional cost will be catastrophic.*

But then, she looked at the two children, who had stopped drawing and were now watching their mother with terrified, mirroring sadness. In that moment, the careful walls of her grief crumbled entirely. The fear was still there, but it was eclipsed by a fierce, protective maternal instinct that she didn't know she possessed. The thought of Lily and Ben spending Christmas night homeless was an unacceptable violation of the season, a cruelty she absolutely had to prevent.

"Get up, Sarah," Grace commanded, her voice steady and decisive, the tone she used when finalizing a complex wedding order. "Go inside. Make those children some cocoa and read them their book. Tell them nothing. I will handle this."

The Secret Transaction

Grace did not go back to her shop. She drove immediately to the bank, her mind racing through the logistics. The total amount due, including the security deposit the landlord had demanded, was staggering—almost eight thousand dollars. It was a sum that Grace could easily cover, but paying it required draining a significant portion of the emergency fund she had established after Tom's death—a fund that represented her carefully guarded **financial security** against a world she deemed unreliable.

More importantly, it meant fully exposing her involvement, which would lead to questions from Sarah, the children, and potentially the whole community. If this huge act of service was known, the secular facade she had so carefully maintained would shatter.

Grace decided on a course of action that was as calculated as it was compassionate: **full payment, absolute secrecy**.

She called the property management company from her car, adopting a false persona—a distant, anonymous benefactor.

"I am acting on behalf of the Miller family at The Mews, Unit B," Grace explained, her voice low and formal. "I understand they have an outstanding balance and are facing eviction. I wish to cover the full back balance, late fees, and the two months' security deposit immediately, via wire transfer."

The property manager, shocked by the size and suddenness of the offer, quickly complied, providing the necessary account information.

Grace made the wire transfer, watching the considerable sum leave her account with a detached sense of finality. It was a deliberate, irreversible step across the boundary she had spent five years defending.

Then, she added two critical, non-negotiable instructions, delivered with the icy precision of a woman who knew exactly what she was buying: **silence and anonymity**.

"I require two things for this transaction to be completed," Grace stated. "One, the eviction notice must be immediately and irrevocably rescinded. Two, under no circumstances is Sarah Miller, or anyone else, to be informed of the source of this payment. It is to be logged as an **anonymous donation** to cover the outstanding balance. If I am identified, I will demand a refund and let the process proceed."

The veiled threat, though empty, was enough. The property manager, motivated by the immediate influx of cash, promised full confidentiality.

Grace hung up the phone, her hands gripping the steering wheel. The deed was done. Sarah and the children were safe for the next few months, their immediate crisis averted. Grace felt a wash of momentary relief, quickly followed by a heavy sense of **isolation**.

She had just performed the largest, most sacrificial act of kindness she had committed since Tom died. She had taken a massive financial and emotional risk, fully investing herself in this family's survival. Yet, she had done it completely alone, driven into the cold, calculated shadows by her refusal to share the motive with the God she still blamed for her pain.

She was performing a **miracle of logistics and finance**, carefully stripped of any religious meaning.

That evening, Grace drove back to The Mews, not with groceries, but with a small, discreetly wrapped toy car for Ben and a new notebook for Lily. She found Sarah already looking slightly less defeated.

"They called me from the property manager's office an hour ago," Sarah said, her eyes still red, but a small spark of hope returning. "The eviction notice was rescinded. They said an anonymous donor covered the entire balance and the security deposit. They said we're safe for the next few months."

Sarah's voice broke on the word "safe." "It has to be a Christmas miracle, Grace. It has to be God."

Grace looked at Sarah, at the children playing quietly on the floor, and felt the immense weight of the secret payment burning within her. The secular contract felt restrictive, suffocating. She was the miracle, but she couldn't claim it, because claiming it would mean having to acknowledge the source of the persistent, selfless compassion that had demanded such sacrifice. It would mean breaking her vow.

"It's good news, Sarah," Grace said simply, meeting the young mother's eyes. "Sometimes, people simply choose to be kind. It doesn't always need a divine explanation. Now, let's get those candles lit. Christmas is almost here."

Grace left The Mews that night, the cold silence of the snowy streets mirroring the cold silence she had imposed upon her own acts of grace. She had solved Sarah's immediate problem, but she had deepened her own spiritual isolation. She was giving everything, yet refusing to admit the truth about the light that compelled her. She was listening to Mrs. Reed's advice—she was talking through her actions—but she was steadfastly refusing to speak a single word to the One who was already listening.

Chapter 5: The Unexpected Blessing

The act of secretly paying **Sarah Miller's** overdue rent and securing their home had provided **Grace Lawson** with a strange, bittersweet sense of peace. She had solved the problem, and in doing so, she had quieted the persistent internal "nudge" that demanded action. By insisting on anonymity, she ensured the act remained entirely secular—a transaction of money and logistics, purely dedicated to **Tom's legacy of human goodness**. Her carefully constructed walls were still standing, albeit significantly breached.

Yet, the proximity to the children, **Lily** and **Ben**, had fundamentally altered her internal landscape. The quiet, profound joy she experienced in their presence was a genuine miracle, a rediscovery of an emotional frequency she believed she had lost forever. With Christmas Day rapidly approaching, Grace realized the sheer emotional impossibility of sending Sarah and the children back to their cold, dark apartment to face the holiday alone.

On the morning of Christmas Eve Eve, the idea surfaced—a spontaneous, reckless spark of warmth. She needed to deep clean and prepare the back workshop of *Bloom & Believe* for the final day of deliveries. The shop was always decorated, of course, but the workshop, filled with discarded pine needles, buckets of murky water, and rolls of wrapping paper, looked purely functional. It needed a touch of frivolous holiday cheer.

Why not invite them here? the thought occurred, bypassing her usual logical filtration system. *I can pay Sarah a small wage for a few hours of holiday help, turning it into a legitimate work arrangement. The children can decorate the back room and stay warm and fed.*

The plan was perfect in its pragmatic disguise. It was a business transaction that provided warmth, food, and a small income for Sarah, while giving Grace the dose of uncomplicated joy she now craved.

Grace called Sarah immediately, keeping her tone strictly professional. "Sarah, I need assistance sorting through some back stock and wrapping supplies this afternoon. It's too cold at The Mews for the children, and frankly, I could use the holiday cheer. I'll pay you hourly. Consider it temporary seasonal help. The children can decorate the workshop, and we'll keep the hot cocoa flowing."

Sarah, overwhelmed and deeply touched by the consistent, unwavering kindness, readily accepted. "Grace, that sounds wonderful. We'll be there. Thank you so much."

Laughter and Lights

That afternoon, the back workshop of *Bloom & Believe* underwent a radical, joyful transformation.

When Sarah, Lily, and Ben arrived, Grace had everything ready: a huge table covered in a plastic drop cloth, boxes filled with unused ribbons, leftover ornaments, strings of colorful lights, and a platter piled high with sugar cookies baked by Grace that morning (another self-confessed act of "inventory management").

The atmosphere instantly shifted from Grace's usual sterile efficiency to one of pure, unrestrained **Christmas chaos**.

Sarah, deeply grateful for the honest work, focused intently on sorting through the ribbons and organizing the wrapping paper. But Lily and Ben, freed from the confines of their small, cold apartment, threw themselves into the decorating task with a zeal Grace hadn't anticipated.

Ben, the five-year-old, decided that the only proper way to hang tinsel was to throw it indiscriminately at the largest, darkest patches of wall, resulting in glistening, chaotic bursts of silver that looked surprisingly festive. Lily, the older child, took on the serious task of stringing lights, carefully winding the multicolored bulbs around buckets of pine branches and stacks of empty flowerpots, transforming the functional workspace into a sparkling, haphazard forest.

Grace found herself simply watching them, leaning against a workbench with a mug of hot cocoa warming her hands. She corrected no one. She fixed no crooked ornaments. She watched as Lily, attempting to reach a high shelf, stretched her arms out wide, her face alight with concentration and triumph. She watched as Ben, completely absorbed in his mission, burst into spontaneous, high-pitched giggles every time a piece of tinsel stuck perfectly to the wall.

The sound of their laughter—unfiltered, bright, and utterly contagious—was a physical balm to Grace's soul. It cut through the five years of silent grief that had encased her heart. It was a sound that had been absent from her home and shop since Tom died, a sound she hadn't realized was a **necessary ingredient for life**.

Sarah, noticing Grace's quiet absorption, stopped working and smiled warmly. "They haven't been this carefree in months, Grace. Honestly, the light in this shop, it's just..." she trailed off, unable to find the words.

"It's just light, Sarah," Grace replied, trying to maintain her detached air. "It's electricity and glass bulbs. It's cheerful, certainly."

"No, I mean the light in *you*," Sarah corrected gently. "I know I don't know you well, but yesterday, you looked so sad, even when you were helping. Today, you're just... present."

Grace instinctively averted her gaze, her cheeks heating slightly at the unexpected intimacy. The truth was undeniable: for the first time in years, she felt **present**. She wasn't replaying the past or dreading the future; she was fully rooted in the messy, joyful *now*.

Lily started singing, a slightly off-key but enthusiastic rendition of "Jingle Bells." Ben immediately joined in, providing loud, rhythmic "Dashing through the snow!" interludes. Soon, Sarah's melodious voice blended with theirs, and the cold workshop was filled with a spontaneous, joyous, a cappella carol.

Grace found herself humming along. Then, tentatively, she allowed herself to sing a quiet harmony line. The feeling was intoxicating. It was the simple, profound joy of togetherness, of shared happiness that asked for nothing in return. It wasn't the solemn, rehearsed joy of the Christmas Eve service she avoided; it was the messy, active, and immediate joy of living.

For Grace, that afternoon was a revelation. It was the stark, undeniable proof that the deep, crippling emotional silence she had endured was a *choice*. She had chosen to mourn in isolation, believing that to feel anything fully—even joy—was a betrayal of her lost love and a risk of future pain. But the children, with their fearless laughter and effortless acceptance, had shown her that her heart was not dead, merely dormant. They had awakened the part of her that Tom had loved best—the part that found solace and beauty in extending compassion.

The Appearance of the Pastor

The joyous session reached its peak when Lily managed to string the final, tangled set of lights across the main window, illuminating the haphazardly decorated workshop in a cascade of warm, chaotic color. Everyone cheered, and Ben took a triumphant, sliding bow.

It was precisely at that moment that the bell on the shop's front door chimed, and **Pastor Daniel Hayes** walked into the main retail area, carrying a large gift basket for Grace.

He paused just inside the threshold of the workshop, taking in the scene: the mountains of paper, the stray tinsel, the buckets of greenery,

Sarah working steadily, and the two children laughing, their small bodies draped over Grace's expensive wool coat as they demanded more cocoa.

Daniel's expression shifted instantly from professional greeting to one of deep, heartfelt pleasure. He had spent five years watching Grace wither under the weight of her grief. Now, for the first time, he was seeing not the successful, guarded businesswoman, but the **woman of purpose** he knew she was meant to be.

"Grace," Daniel began, his voice filled with genuine warmth. "This is a magnificent surprise. I came to drop off a small Christmas token, but I seem to have stumbled into the North Pole's unofficial outreach program."

He walked over to Grace, greeting Sarah and the children kindly. "These are beautiful works," he told Lily, admiring the tangled string of lights with sincere appreciation.

Grace immediately felt the familiar, cold surge of **exposure**. The sheer, public nature of this encounter threatened to collapse her secular facade. Daniel was a man of faith; he would instantly recognize her actions as the fulfillment of the very purpose she denied.

"Pastor Daniel," Grace said, rising quickly, pulling her coat around her like a shield. "Please don't misunderstand. This is not... a ministry. Sarah is helping me with a huge amount of backstock organization for a few hours. I am paying her fair wage, and the children are helping with *decorating* the chaos."

She emphasized the words *wage* and *decorating*—the functional, transactional language of commerce. She needed Daniel to understand that this was a professional engagement, not a spiritual rebirth.

Daniel, sensing the familiar tension, softened his gaze and stepped closer, keeping his voice low so only she could hear. "Grace, you don't need to categorize your kindness for me. I know what I'm seeing."

He gestured with his hand, encompassing the laughing children, the warm light, and the immense peace that seemed to radiate from Grace's usually guarded posture.

"I see the **good works** that James wrote about," Daniel continued gently, referencing the Epistle of James, which speaks of faith being demonstrated through action. "I see a woman who chose to warm the cold, feed the hungry, and offer employment and dignity when others failed to see the need."

Grace bristled, her voice hardening with the familiar, defensive resentment. "I repeat, Pastor, I am not doing this for **God**. I am doing this for Sarah. I am doing this for the children. I am simply fulfilling my duty as a member of this community to help those who are struggling. It's basic human ethics. It's a way to keep Tom's memory alive through action. It has absolutely nothing to do with the Church or the silence I received five years ago."

The mention of the "silence" was rare, a raw wound she almost never exposed. She watched Daniel closely, expecting the usual religious platitudes about God's plan or mysterious ways.

Daniel looked directly into her eyes, his own filled with compassion, and did not offer a platitude. Instead, he acknowledged her truth, subtly reframing it.

"I understand your pain, Grace, and I will never minimize what you lost," he said sincerely. "But you can insist that you are simply 'helping'—and that is profoundly true. However, perhaps the definition of 'helping' is much broader than you allow. When you perform an act of love—whether you call it ethics, duty, or human goodness—you are participating in something far older and greater than your own grief."

He paused, letting the weight of his words settle. "You have stopped talking to God, Grace, but He hasn't stopped talking to you. He speaks through the laughter of these children. He speaks through the warmth of this room. And He speaks through the impulse in your heart that forced you to drive to The Mews. You can call it whatever you want, but I assure you, your **compassion is His signature.**"

He didn't press her further. He simply handed her the gift basket, gave her a warm, supportive look, and walked away, the bell chiming quietly behind him.

The Weight of Joy

Daniel's words—*your compassion is His signature*—stayed with Grace long after he left. They were the perfect, gentle counter-argument to her tightly controlled secular narrative. She had built her walls against the Divine, but she couldn't deny the inherent, selfless goodness that kept breaking through those walls.

The rest of the afternoon was saturated with warmth and activity. As darkness fell outside, the colorful lights in the workshop cast a magical, haphazard glow. They ate a simple, early dinner of takeout pizza, which tasted like the most exquisite feast, punctuated by Ben's sticky, high-fives and Lily's detailed description of her favorite ornament.

As the time approached for them to return home, a genuine, profound weariness settled over Grace—not the exhaustion of grief, but the deep, satisfying fatigue of a day well-spent in active love.

"Thank you, Grace," Sarah said, gathering her children. "This was the best day we've had in a year. Thank you for making us feel welcome."

"It was necessary, Sarah," Grace insisted, handing Sarah the promised cash payment, doubling it discreetly without comment. "The shop is organized, and the energy you brought here was invaluable. I'll see you tomorrow."

After they left, the workshop fell silent, illuminated only by the strings of chaotic, multicolored lights. Grace stood in the quiet room, the lingering scent of cocoa and pine clinging to the air, and felt the immense weight of the truth.

The joy she had experienced that afternoon—the sheer, uncomplicated pleasure of communal warmth and purpose—was unlike anything she had felt in five years. It was **healing**. It was **renewal**. It was exactly what she had refused to pray for, but exactly what had been delivered.

She knew, with a sudden, devastating clarity, that her continued involvement with Sarah was no longer merely about honoring Tom. It was about **saving herself**. Tom's legacy was the catalyst, but the healing was happening directly to her.

She walked over to the workbench, running her fingers over a small, carved wooden star that Lily had used to prop up a ribbon spool. It was simple, imperfect, and made with true intention—just like the star Tom had given her years ago, the one he said represented hope.

Grace realized that the very *act* of selfless service was a form of worship, regardless of the words she refused to speak. She was engaged in the divine conversation, not through spoken prayer, but through demonstrable compassion.

That night, as she lay in the silence of her own perfectly warm, perfectly lonely bedroom, she felt the **nudge** return—no longer a pressure of guilt, but a gentle, undeniable pull of **belonging**. She hadn't surrendered her will, but her heart had been softened and renewed by the unexpected blessing of light, laughter, and an honest day's work. She had insisted that she was just "helping," but the emotional evidence now pointed to a profound, unsolicited **miracle**.

Chapter 6: The Night of Need

Christmas Eve was traditionally the quietest day for **Grace Lawson's** personal life, a sterile vacuum she usually filled with meticulous post-holiday inventory planning. This year, however, the silence was shattered long before dusk.

The afternoon had been deceptively peaceful. After closing *Bloom & Believe* early, Grace found herself sitting in her warm kitchen, feeling a strange mix of anticipation and dread. Her heart, so recently warmed by the company of **Sarah, Lily, and Ben**, now felt the hollowness of their absence acutely. She was fighting the urge to call them, to invent another "inventory surplus" reason for them to return. She knew she was becoming dangerously attached, relying on their uncomplicated joy to sustain her fragile sense of purpose.

The frantic ring of her landline around seven o'clock cut through the quiet, and Grace answered with an immediate, deep premonition.

"Grace? Auntie Grace, please, you have to come!"

It was **Lily**, the eight-year-old, her voice high and thin with panic, punctuated by the whimpering sound of **Ben** in the background.

"Lily, calm down. It's Grace. What's wrong? Where's your mother?" Grace demanded, her professional calm instantly returning, overriding the shock.

"Mommy is really sick! She fell down, and she's hot, but she's shaking so bad, and she won't wake up right," Lily explained, her words tumbling out in a rush. "She made us promise not to call an ambulance, she said it costs too much money, but she's scared, Grace. She looks scared."

The mention of the ambulance costs—Sarah's fierce, desperate protection of her financial safety net—twisted a knife in Grace's chest. The crisis was no longer about hunger or cold; it was about **life and death**, a reality that immediately stripped away Grace's carefully constructed defenses. She knew, with a terrible certainty, that this was the moment her secular kindness met its ultimate test. This required total surrender to vulnerability.

"Listen to me, Lily. You are so brave," Grace said, already grabbing her car keys and coat. "Do not hang up. Go to the door and unlock it right now. Tell Ben to sit quietly. I am driving to you, and I will be there in four minutes. I promise. Keep talking to me until I get there."

The Crisis Point

The drive to The Mews was a terrifying blur. The snow had begun to fall again, heavy and thick, turning the twinkling lights of Main Street into hazy, impressionistic blobs. Grace kept Lily on the phone, receiving a breathless, terrified play-by-play of the apartment.

When she burst through the unlocked door, the scene was worse than she had imagined. The space heater was struggling, but the air was still cold. Sarah lay crumpled on the worn sofa, covered in sweat despite the chill, her breathing shallow and ragged. Lily was standing over her, clutching a wet, cold washcloth, her small face streaked with tears. Ben was curled into a ball in the corner, whimpering quietly, watching the unfolding drama with wide, frightened eyes.

Grace dropped her bag and rushed immediately to Sarah's side. She felt Sarah's forehead—it was burning hot, the skin clammy.

"She's delirious, Lily," Grace murmured, already checking for any visible injuries from the fall. Grace wasn't a medical professional, but years of managing the risks of a busy flower shop had given her a practical competence in crisis management. She realized Sarah was gripped by a severe, sudden fever—likely the flu, or perhaps worse, a reaction to the persistent cold and stress.

"I need you to be my assistant, Lily. Can you do that?" Grace asked, meeting the girl's frantic gaze.

Lily nodded fiercely, eager for a task. "Yes, Auntie Grace. Anything."

Grace quickly gave instructions: Lily was to retrieve the spare blankets and boil water for tea. Grace assessed the situation. Sarah was too ill to move, and Grace could not risk taking her to the hospital without Sarah's consent, knowing the financial terror it would unleash. She had to manage the fever and the dehydration here, now, in the stillness of this cold, lonely room.

Grace gently moved Sarah into a more comfortable position, immediately forcing small sips of water into her, speaking in soft, continuous tones. She worked through the long evening and into the night, managing the fever with methodical, tireless dedication. She rotated cold compresses, administered fever reducer she kept in her own car emergency kit, and kept talking to Sarah in low, soothing tones, urging her to drink, breathe, and rest.

The hours bled together in the dimly lit apartment, broken only by the crackle of the inadequate space heater and the rhythmic sound of Sarah's labored breathing.

The Quiet in the Middle of the Night

Around 3:00 AM, the crisis seemed to stabilize. Sarah finally succumbed to a deep, restorative sleep, the oppressive fever having broken slightly, leaving her skin cool and damp. Lily and Ben, exhausted by the day's panic and reassured by Grace's steady, capable presence, had fallen asleep, huddled together under the new reindeer blanket on the floor near the struggling heater.

Grace sat beside the sofa, finally allowing herself to rest. The apartment was profoundly silent, save for the gentle rhythm of three healthy breaths. It was Christmas Day now—the day the entire town of Evergreen Valley celebrated the miracle of the Christ Child.

Grace was physically and emotionally spent, having fought off a terrifying illness with sheer will and practical love. She looked around the small, impoverished room, illuminated by the distant, soft glow of the town's lights filtering through the dingy windowpane. She looked at the children, their faces serene in sleep, and then at Sarah, who was finally resting without the tremor of fever.

In that profound, holy quiet, alone with the profound reality of human fragility and the tangible evidence of her own exhausted, tireless kindness, **Grace's walls finally collapsed**.

The moment was devoid of the theatrical demand for a miracle that had defined her prayer five years ago. There was no desperate bargaining, no attempt to dictate the outcome. This was simple, raw **surrender**.

She bowed her head, not over a Bible, but over her own cold, tired hands. She did not kneel, but she was more prostate than she had ever been. She did not speak with the eloquence of the church hymns, but with the stark, trembling sincerity of a soul broken open by love and fear.

She began to **pray again**—unsure, hesitant, the words rusty on her tongue.

"*Father,*" she whispered, the title feeling foreign and yet intensely familiar. "*I... I don't know if you're listening. I don't know if You ever listen. I'm not asking You to heal her instantly. I'm not asking You for a show of power. I'm asking only for help.*"

Tears, hot and unexpected, streamed down her face. They were not tears of grief for Tom, but tears of fear for Sarah and the children, and tears of profound, desperate **humility** for herself.

"*I have done everything I know how to do,*" Grace continued, her voice thick with emotion. "*I fought the fever, I gave the medication, I kept them warm. But I am just a florist, Lord. I am limited. I am so tired.*"

She finally confessed the truth she had guarded for five years. "*I blamed You for Tom. I walked away. I told myself I didn't need You, that human goodness was enough. But tonight, I'm afraid. If she takes a turn, if I can't stop this, those children lose everything, and I lose the only reason my heart has come back to life.*"

The words were raw, unpolished, and completely honest. She was not praying for a theological answer; she was praying for **support**. She was admitting her weakness and, in doing so, finally acknowledging the existence of a strength greater than her own resources.

"*If You are still the God of Tom, the God of purpose, and the God who sees the vulnerable,*" she whispered into the silence of the room, "*then please. Be here. Hold us. Help her survive this night. And if You help us, I promise, I will stop fighting You. I will try to talk to You again.*"

She finished the prayer, not with a flourish of resolution, but with a deep, shaky sigh of exhaustion. She waited, expecting the cold, crushing silence of five years ago.

But this time, the silence was different. It was not empty or indifferent. It was **profoundly, intensely peaceful**.

It was the quiet stillness that follows a violent storm, the profound sense of **rest** and **assurance** that settled over the apartment. Grace felt an immediate, tangible shift in the atmosphere—not a miracle of action, but a miracle of **presence**. She felt held, not just in the physical reality of the small room, but in the spiritual reality of the universe. The relentless, internal pressure she had felt since helping Sarah finally lifted, replaced by a deep, enduring sense of **solace**.

Peace Like the Dawn

Grace did not sleep, but she rested deeply, watching over her makeshift family. As the first pale, rosy light of Christmas morning touched the snow outside, she felt the last vestiges of her emotional exhaustion receding.

At six o'clock, Sarah stirred, her eyes fluttering open. Her gaze focused on Grace, sitting beside her.

"Grace?" Sarah's voice was weak, but clear, without the frantic delirium of the night before. "The children… are they alright?"

"They are fine, Sarah. They're asleep," Grace replied softly, immediately checking Sarah's temperature one last time. The fever was gone. It was a normal temperature, the kind of gentle, complete reversal that speaks less of coincidence and more of **providence** and **restored vitality**.

Sarah closed her eyes and offered a silent, private prayer of thanks, a simple expression of gratitude that Grace now understood completely.

When Sarah opened her eyes again, she looked at Grace with a love and comprehension that transcended their brief acquaintance. "You stayed the whole night. You saved us. I don't know what I would have done."

"We're safe now," Grace insisted, a quiet, unfamiliar **peace** flooding her heart.

The peace was the final, undeniable sign. It wasn't the fleeting satisfaction of a good deed, or the temporary relief of avoiding disaster. It was the enduring, steady calm that comes from **reconciliation**. Grace realized that the "miracle" of that night wasn't Sarah's physical healing—which could be attributed to rest and medication—but the fact that Grace had been driven to a point of such utter vulnerability that she had no choice but to lay down her weapons and **speak to God again**.

The fever had passed, but something far deeper and more insidious had also broken: **Grace's paralyzing self-reliance.** She was no longer just helping; she was **serving** from a place of open, trusting, though still nascent, faith. The silence had been broken, not by a boom of thunder, but by the quiet, still voice of **assurance** that filled the room after her trembling, honest plea.

As the children began to stir, Grace felt the peace settle into the deepest parts of her soul. She had asked God for help in the night, and in return, she had received the one thing she desperately needed:

the comforting knowledge that she was **not alone** in her struggle. The battle was over, and in the stillness of that humble room on Christmas morning, Grace had found her way back to the conversation.

Chapter 7: The Miracle in the Mail

The day after Christmas was characterized by a profound, yet precarious **peace** that settled over **Grace Lawson**. She had returned **Sarah Miller** and the children to their apartment early that morning, ensuring Sarah saw a doctor for a non-emergency follow-up (covered, of course, by Grace as an "advanced payment for future assistance"). The fever was gone, the exhaustion remained, but the terrifying crisis was over.

For Grace, the physical weariness was eclipsed by a deep spiritual fatigue—the exhaustion of having fought, lost, and surrendered. Her trembling, fearful prayer in the middle of the night had been answered, not with a booming voice or a dramatic healing, but with a simple, unmistakable **solace** that had filled the quiet room. It was the calm assurance that she was not carrying the burden alone. She had broken her vow of silence, and in that moment of surrender, her heart had been granted a reprieve.

She spent the subsequent days managing the end-of-year rush at *Bloom & Believe* with a mechanical competence, her movements efficient but distant. She was trying desperately to rationalize the peace she felt. Was it merely the psychological relief of a crisis averted? Was it the exhaustion of the vigil? Or was it, as **Pastor Daniel Hayes** had suggested, the unmistakable **signature** of a God who responds to need, regardless of the petitioner's doubt?

Grace clung to the practical, the visible. She focused on the tangible truth: Sarah and the children were safe, warm, and fed, and that was the result of *her* actions, dedicated to *Tom's memory*. She pushed the profound, spiritual peace she had felt into a dusty corner of her mind, treating it like an abstract emotion that needed to be ignored in favor of the concrete reality of roses and ribbons.

The Anonymous Delivery

It was December 28th, a cold, grey afternoon typical of late New England winter. Grace was in her private office, meticulously reconciling the year-end accounts. She was facing the stark figures that reflected her large, secret contribution to Sarah's rent—the nearly **eight thousand dollars** that had drained her emergency fund and terrified her with its sudden vulnerability. She was just calculating the amount she needed to replenish the fund in the new year when her assistant brought in the day's mail.

"Just bills and flyers, Grace, except for this," the assistant said, setting a small stack of envelopes on the desk. She tapped one item specifically. "This was hand-delivered. No stamp, just placed in the box."

Grace picked up the item. It was a heavy, cream-colored envelope, sealed not with commercial glue, but with a small dollop of dark red wax stamped with an intricate, floral design. The envelope was entirely **anonymous**. There was no return address, and her name, "Grace Lawson," was written in elegant, looping script by an unfamiliar hand.

A knot of profound unease tightened in Grace's stomach. Her world of floral design and civic duty was orderly and professional. This envelope felt like something out of a period drama, too formal and secretive for Evergreen Valley.

She carefully broke the wax seal, her fingers surprisingly steady despite the sudden spike of adrenaline. Inside, she found two items:

1. A crisp, perfectly folded linen note card.
2. A thick stack of banded US currency.

Grace's breath caught in her throat. She stared at the bills, her mind struggling to process the visual information. The stack was neatly bundled into large denominations. She counted them quickly, her hands shaking slightly—they totaled exactly **$8,000.**

It was the precise, overwhelming amount she had secretly wired to the property management company to prevent Sarah's eviction.

Her focus shifted to the note card, the feeling of disbelief so intense it bordered on vertigo. Her eyes scanned the elegant script, which offered the devastatingly specific words that brought her secular walls crashing down around her.

The message read:

Because you gave in secret, Heaven saw in full. Keep believing.

The Impossibility of Knowledge

Grace reread the note three times, her mind grasping desperately for a logical, rational explanation. The words were simple, yet they were an impossible intrusion into her most guarded secret.

Because you gave in secret.

Only three people in the entire world knew about that payment: Grace herself, the property manager, and the banker who handled the wire transfer. The property manager had promised absolute, iron-clad anonymity under threat of Grace demanding a refund—a threat the manager would not dare breach, especially not to anonymously return the money. The banker had no knowledge of *why* the transfer was made, only that it was to a property company.

And most critically, the note didn't say, *"Because you were generous."* It said, *"Because you gave **in secret.**"* It targeted the single most defining characteristic of the payment: Grace's need for isolation and anonymity, her refusal to allow the kindness to be attributed to the faith she had abandoned.

The secular explanation—the human, logical answer—simply did not exist.

Her heart began to pound with a frantic energy. This wasn't a coincidence. This wasn't a friend guessing. This was a direct, undeniable confirmation that the payment she had made in the cold, transactional shadows had been **witnessed by something outside the boundaries of her control.**

Her carefully constructed theory—that her compassion was purely an act of "human ethics" honoring Tom—had just been obliterated by an anonymous envelope containing the exact sum of her sacrifice.

Grace spent the next hour in a frenzy of investigation. She called the property manager again, her voice tight and demanding.

"Did you, or anyone in your office, divulge the payment amount, the timing, or the anonymous nature of the Miller rent payment?"

The manager, clearly frightened by the intensity of Grace's tone, emphatically denied everything. "Ms. Lawson, I promise you, that file is sealed. No one has seen it. We marked it as an *anonymous community contribution*. I have upheld our agreement completely."

Grace knew the manager was telling the truth; the fear in his voice was genuine. She then drove to The Mews, desperately hoping to find some clue. She questioned Sarah casually, asking if anyone had approached her with bizarre questions or anonymous gifts.

"No, Grace. Nothing strange," Sarah replied, folding laundry. "Just the beautiful calm. The fear is gone. It was a Christmas miracle, Grace. God saw us struggling and intervened."

Sarah's simple, unshakeable faith in divine intervention only intensified Grace's internal crisis. Grace knew *she* was the one who had intervened, but now, someone *else*—or something *else*—was intervening with *her*.

She drove back to her shop, the stack of money and the linen note card burning a hole in her passenger seat. The reality was inescapable: she had performed a massive, secret, financial sacrifice to maintain her secular facade, and in response, the money had been returned, accompanied by a note that proved the act was **fully seen** by a witness who operated outside of human rules.

The prayer she had whispered in the dark night of crisis—the tentative, broken plea for help—had been answered not just with peace, but with this blinding, material confirmation.

The Signature of Compassion

Utterly defeated, Grace realized she could no longer handle the information alone. She knew where she had to go. She drove straight to **Pastor Daniel Hayes's** study, finding him preparing for the New Year's service.

She walked into his office without knocking, collapsing into a leather chair. She didn't speak; she simply placed the envelope, the money, and the linen note card on his desk.

Daniel looked at the thick stack of cash, then at the elegant wax-sealed envelope, and finally, he read the note: *"Because you gave in secret, Heaven saw in full. Keep believing."*

He looked up at Grace, his face unreadable, completely devoid of judgment or surprise.

"Tell me everything, Grace," he commanded, his voice soft, yet carrying an immense authority.

Grace, no longer defensive, poured out the entire five-week saga: the guilt, the secret eight-thousand-dollar payment, the financial terror, the fearful prayer in the middle of the night, and the shame she felt at using Tom's legacy as a substitute for faith. She confessed her anger, her doubt, and her profound sense of having been abandoned.

When she finished, the room was silent. The only sound was the faint hiss of the radiator and the rustle of the linen note card Daniel held gently between his fingers.

"And you are absolutely certain, Grace, that no one knew the amount, or the anonymity of the transaction?" he asked, confirming the impossibility.

"No one, Daniel. I threatened the property manager into silence. This is impossible. It is a mathematical and logistical impossibility," Grace insisted, her voice raw.

Daniel nodded slowly, placing the note card back on the desk next to the returned money. He settled back in his chair, his gaze full of the gentle, profound wisdom she had sought from **Mrs. Reed**, but now layered with a knowledge of the divine.

"This is not magic, Grace. This is not coincidence," Daniel stated, his voice quiet but firm. "This is confirmation. You were so determined to keep your action secular and private that you were terrified of the world finding out. But you forgot that there is an **Audience of One** who sees every act of pure, selfless love."

He leaned forward, meeting her gaze. "In the dark night, Grace, when you were exhausted and terrified, you said, 'If You are still the God of Tom... help her survive this night.' That prayer wasn't about Tom's life anymore. It was about **your life's purpose**. You weren't demanding a miracle, you were pleading for support."

Daniel reached out and gently nudged the stack of eight thousand dollars.

"This," he said, his voice ringing with quiet conviction, "is God's way of ensuring that your obedience is not penalized. You sacrificed your financial security to help the widow and the orphans, and He has returned your security in full, with a written message that proves He witnessed the act."

He delivered the final, life-changing interpretation that connected her spiritual despair to her present reality.

"You asked God for the miracle of Tom's life, and He had to say no, which felt like silence. You were then silent to Him for five years, but He was never silent to you. And now, you whispered a prayer of surrender, and He has answered—not with what you asked for five years ago, but with **exactly what you needed now**: confirmation that

He sees you, He knows your secret pain, and He trusts you with the next task."

Daniel picked up the note card one last time, reading the final line. *"Keep believing."*

"**God just answered your prayer—not with what you asked for, but what you needed,**" Daniel concluded. "He needed you to know that the compassion in your heart is not your enemy, and that the only true reward is the certainty that He knows you by name."

Grace looked at the money, the note, and then at Daniel, and for the first time since the night in the apartment, her peace was not fragile. It was **concrete**. It was backed by eight thousand undeniable dollars and the simple, impossible truth of the written word. Her spiritual journey had begun again, baptized by the overwhelming evidence of grace.

Chapter 8: The Light Returns

The revelation delivered in the anonymous, wax-sealed envelope—the precise, impossible return of **eight thousand dollars**—did what five years of grief, logic, and self-recrimination could not: it shattered **Grace Lawson's** secular barricade and forced her into the terrifying, exhilarating reality of divine attention.

The money, the physical proof of a witnessed, secret act of compassion, was placed immediately back into her emergency savings fund. It was no longer a symbol of financial security against a cruel world; it was a **deposit of trust**, a profound promise that her obedience would not result in her ruin. The accompanying note—*"Because you gave in secret, Heaven saw in full. Keep believing."*—had become her new, private scripture, a direct command to shed her isolation and fully embrace the purpose she had tried to relegate to Tom's memory.

The internal conflict was over. The **light** that had begun as a fragile flicker—triggered by Ben's tears and sustained by Lily's laughter—was now demanding to be an open flame.

Grace spent the last three days of the old year talking openly with **Sarah Miller**. This time, the conversation was free of professional distance and transactional pretenses. Grace confessed the immense financial sacrifice she had made, explaining the impossible return of the money as the final, humbling catalyst for her change of heart. Sarah, whose faith was simple and direct, listened with awe, confirming

Grace's own emerging belief that they had been part of a genuine, tangible miracle.

"It wasn't just a miracle for us, Grace," Sarah said, sitting in Grace's bright, warm kitchen. "It was a miracle for you. He used our cold and our fear to get through your walls. And now that you're back in the light, we have to share it."

The shared purpose solidified instantly: they would host a belated **Christmas dinner** for the forgotten families of Evergreen Valley. The town's official festivities had concluded, and the general cheer had subsided, leaving the struggling families once again facing the stark reality of winter poverty and post-holiday debt. They would call it the **Feast of the Epiphany**—a light to the world, a new beginning.

A New Purpose for Bloom & Believe

The venue was instantly clear: *Bloom & Believe*. Grace's beautiful, historic flower shop, with its high ceilings, original wood floors, and overwhelming scent of fresh pine and eucalyptus, would be transformed from a place of commerce into a **sanctuary of fellowship**.

Grace threw herself into the logistics, but this time, her efficiency was fueled not by guilt or obligation, but by boundless, selfless joy. She saw the eight thousand dollars in her account not as a cushion, but as **working capital for grace**. She spent freely, buying mountains of food, durable plasticware, children's books, and—most importantly—two dozen small, high-quality space heaters and heavy blankets, items she knew were vital for families living in the unheated corners of The Mews.

Sarah, now her full partner and coordinator, was invaluable. She knew the families, she knew the specific needs, and she knew how to extend an invitation with dignity and respect. The focus was simple: a warm room, a hot, abundant meal, and the shared realization that they were **seen and loved**.

Word spread quietly, guided by Sarah's gentle discretion and Pastor Daniel's enthusiastic, though carefully managed, support. The dinner was set for the evening of January 5th.

The afternoon of the dinner, *Bloom & Believe* was virtually unrecognizable. All the delicate retail displays were moved to the perimeter. The central space was filled with long, borrowed banquet tables covered in crisp white linen. Grace refused to buy new flowers; instead, the tables were decorated with rustic centerpieces of pine cones, cedar boughs, and simple white pillar candles, lending the room a clean, humble elegance.

The scent was intoxicating—a mix of roasting chicken, mashed potatoes, fresh-baked bread, and the lingering fragrance of the shop's winter stock. Sarah, radiant with renewed hope and purpose, supervised the food distribution, while Lily and Ben, dressed in their warmest holiday clothes, became the official greeters and seat managers, guiding timid families to the best spots near the portable heating units Grace had installed.

Grace stood near the entrance, greeting each family personally. She saw the familiar anxiety in their eyes—the defensive posture of people used to receiving charity. But as they stepped inside, the sheer, abundant warmth and the rich aroma of the feast seemed to melt their reserve. They saw not a formal soup kitchen, but a beautiful, brightly lit home.

The shop quickly filled with nearly fifty people: single mothers, elderly couples, laid-off fathers, and a swarm of children. The air, heavy with the scent of dinner, was soon filled with the loud, chaotic **sound of laughter**—the sound Grace had missed for so long. Lily and Ben, knowing almost every child by name, immediately drew them into games of hide-and-seek among the towering racks of ribbons, their joy an infectious antidote to the adult worry in the room.

Grace moved seamlessly through the room, her heart aching with a familiar, yet now welcome, pain—the profound joy of **selfless**

connection. She saw a young mother weep softly when she realized there were seconds and thirds available. She watched an older gentleman warm his gnarled hands over one of the ceramic heaters. She saw the children devour the mashed potatoes, their faces smeared with butter and pure, uninhibited happiness.

This was what Tom had meant. This was the **pain of purpose**. It was exhausting, overwhelming, and utterly complete.

The Light of the Word

When the main meal was finished, and the remnants of the feast were being quietly cleared, Pastor Daniel, who had been sitting quietly at a corner table, stood up. His presence was not intimidating; he was simply a part of the fellowship, a quiet servant.

"Friends," Daniel said, his voice carrying over the din. "Before we share dessert, I want to invite us all into a moment of thanks and reflection. We are gathered in this beautiful place because the light of a single, secret act of love broke through the darkness of this past month."

He paused, his eyes finding Grace's across the room, offering a subtle nod of recognition and affection.

"Grace, my dear," Daniel continued, "the last few weeks have been a testament to the power of a life renewed. Would you honor us by reading the original story that reminds us why we share warmth and light on a cold night?"

The request struck Grace with the force of a divine command. Reading the scriptures had been her favorite role in the church until Tom's death. She had silently, fiercely vowed never to utter those words in public again, fearing they would summon the bitter memories of her unanswered prayers.

Now, she had no refuge. The room was warm, filled with the vulnerable people she had chosen to serve, and the light of expectation was on her. She felt the heavy silence settle over the room, an expectant hush that demanded her truth.

She walked slowly to the small, decorated table where Daniel had placed a small, worn Bible. She picked it up, her fingers trembling slightly as they felt the leather cover—the same texture as the Bible she had abandoned on her own shelf. She found the familiar passage instantly: **Luke 2: The Nativity.**

She cleared her throat, her voice catching on the first attempt. The trembling was not just in her hand; it was deep in her chest, the residual fear of vulnerability.

"I... I apologize," Grace whispered, looking down at the text, seeing not just letters, but the ghost of Tom's smiling face as he would have read the passage himself, his voice booming with faith.

She took a deep breath, recalling the feeling of **peace** from the night of need, the absolute certainty of **solace** she had received when she finally surrendered. She lifted her chin and began to read.

"*And it came to pass in those days, that there went out a decree from Caesar Augustus, that all the world should be taxed...*"

Her voice, initially a dry, shaking whisper, quickly gained strength. As she progressed through the familiar story—the journey to Bethlehem, the crowded inn, the simple birth in the stable—the sound of her own voice reciting the holy narrative felt like the final act of **reconciliation**. Every word was an argument against the grief and bitterness she had nursed for so long. Every comma was a breath of renewed acceptance.

When she reached the climactic moment, her voice was strong, clear, and filled with a luminous, unmistakable **joy.**

"*And the angel said unto them, Fear not: for, behold, I bring you* **good tidings of great joy,** *which shall be to all people.*"

She continued, reading about the multitude of the heavenly host, the shepherds, and the profound, humble peace that settled over the world. As she read the final verses, describing Mary pondering these things in her heart, Grace felt the return of her **faith** not as a sudden lightning bolt, but as the quiet, slow, and undeniable certainty of **dawn breaking** over a landscape long shrouded in night.

The fear was gone. The resentment was replaced by gratitude. She had walked away from the light, but the light, manifesting first as a mother and her children, and then as eight thousand returned dollars, had inexorably led her back home.

Grace closed the Bible, the sound a quiet, final period on five years of isolation. She looked up at the room full of people—the hungry, the cold, the vulnerable—and saw them not as problems to be solved, but as the **evidence of her purpose**.

The **light had returned** not just to *Bloom & Believe*, but to Grace Lawson's heart, a gentle, powerful radiance fueled by the love she had risked and the God who had seen her secret sacrifice in full. The conversation was not only restored; it was thriving, celebrated in the shared laughter, the rich aroma of food, and the undeniable presence of grace in the heart of her simple flower shop.

The true miracle wasn't the Christmas Eve healing, or the money; it was the fact that a broken, angry woman had found the courage to love again, and in doing so, had found her way back to the love that created her.

Chapter 9: A Miracle at Christmas

The calendar pages had turned with breathtaking speed, marking the passage of a full, transformative year since the Feast of the Epiphany dinner in **Grace Lawson's** flower shop. The relentless, deep winter had given way to the soft promise of spring, transitioned through the vibrant chaos of summer weddings, and settled once more into the quiet, crystalline silence of a New England Christmas.

The changes in Evergreen Valley were visible, but the changes in Grace were profound. *Bloom & Believe* was no longer just a shop; it had become the unofficial hub of a burgeoning community outreach effort. With the returned eight thousand dollars as seed money—a fund Grace now called the "Deposit of Trust"—she and **Sarah Miller** had founded a small, informal non-profit dedicated to bridging the gaps in emergency aid for local families facing eviction or heating crises. Sarah, now employed part-time at the shop and full-time as the non-profit's coordinator, managed the intake, offering aid with the fierce, protective empathy born of her own past struggle.

Lily and Ben were thriving. Ben, now six, was in the first grade, a cheerful, talkative boy who still called Grace "Auntie Grace" and spent every Saturday morning in her sun-drenched kitchen, assisting with cookie dough and learning the names of exotic ferns. Lily, nine, was a focused, capable girl whose artwork now decorated the walls of the back office, filling the space with color and uncomplicated joy. They were, in every sense, Grace's family.

Grace's faith had matured from a fragile, confirmed theory into a quiet, enduring reality. She still missed **Tom** with an aching, physical depth, but the memory was no longer encased in bitterness. It was a soft, steady **blessing**—the foundation upon which her new life of service was built. She understood now that Tom's love had been the catalyst, but God's grace had been the power source, forcing her back into the light through the simple, undeniable need of others.

On this particular night, **Christmas Eve**, the air was sharp and cold, carrying the faint scent of woodsmoke and freshly fallen snow. Grace, dressed simply in a deep emerald dress, locked the shop for the last time that year. She felt a peaceful anticipation, an emotional completeness that surpassed any joy she had known, even before Tom's death. She was not just *attending* the service tonight; she was *belonging* to it.

The Silent Sanctuary

The First Presbyterian Church of Evergreen Valley was a masterpiece of classic New England architecture—white clapboard, tall spire, and large, arched windows that glowed warmly against the twilight. Inside, the space was filled with the collective hush of hundreds of people gathered in expectation. Cedar garlands draped the balcony railings, and the large pipe organ hummed a low, reverent undertone.

Grace found her usual pew—the one three rows back, slightly off-center—the same pew she had sat in for twenty years with Tom, and the same one she had avoided for five years after his death. Tonight, she sat flanked by her new family: Sarah on one side, radiant and composed, and Lily and Ben, scrubbed clean and quiet with the seriousness of the hour, perched close to her on the other.

Pastor Daniel Hayes stood at the pulpit, his face grave and reflective as he welcomed the congregation. He spoke briefly about the passing of the year, the cyclical nature of hope and darkness, and the profound human need for a light greater than our own strength.

Then, Daniel shifted the focus. "Tonight," he said, his voice lowering with sincerity, "we do not just reflect on a historical event. We look for the evidence of God's plan in our own lives, today, in our own community. Because the truest miracles often happen in the quiet moments, in the secret sacrifices that change the world one family at a time."

He then announced the special part of the service. "This year, we have asked one of our own—a woman whose life was profoundly touched by such a secret sacrifice exactly one year ago—to share her **testimony**. Please welcome Sarah Miller."

A collective intake of breath rustled through the congregation. Sarah, her hands steady, her eyes shining with controlled emotion, rose and walked to the front. Grace watched her go, feeling a tremor of nervous pride, knowing that this was Sarah's moment, the public affirmation of the faith that had been born in cold, desperate need.

Sarah's Testimony: The Stranger's Kindness

Sarah stood at the pulpit, her posture straight and dignified, holding a small microphone. The warmth of the lights emphasized the lines of fatigue that still faintly shadowed her face, signs of the difficult journey she had traveled.

"A year ago tonight, I was sitting on the steps of my apartment building with an **eviction notice** in my hands," Sarah began, her voice clear and strong, yet threaded with the fragility of memory. "It was forty-eight hours before Christmas, and I knew I had nowhere to take my children. I had failed. I had been working every hour I could, but the late fees and the debt from the months before had piled up, and the amount they demanded to stop the eviction was impossible. It was almost eight thousand dollars."

She paused, letting the staggering number sink in for the audience—a figure that represented security to many, but utter ruin to her.

"I was broken," she continued, recounting the terror. "I felt that familiar shame—that feeling that my children would be taken away, that the universe was indifferent to our struggle. I called a friend, the friend who had been helping us with small things—groceries, blankets. She was the only human lifeline I had left, and she was already spread thin."

Sarah's eyes swept over the congregation, meeting many sympathetic gazes, but she avoided Grace entirely, maintaining the dramatic integrity of the narrative.

"That friend told me to go inside, keep the children warm, and wait. And I did. I waited, and I wept, and I prayed the only prayer I had left: 'Lord, if You see us, if You truly see the widow and the orphan, please, send us a sign.' I did not pray for money. I prayed for a sign that **we were seen**."

"The next morning," Sarah's voice swelled slightly, "I received a call from the property manager. They were confused, almost hesitant. They told me that the entire balance—all the back rent, all the late fees, and the security deposit—had been covered. **Eight thousand dollars** had been wired to their account, and the eviction was immediately, irrevocably rescinded."

A wave of quiet murmuring moved through the church. People exchanged astonished glances; the scale of the private donation was immense, even for a community as tight-knit as Evergreen Valley.

"When I asked who did this," Sarah continued, her voice filled with awe, "the manager was firm. They said the donor had provided the money under the strictest, non-negotiable condition of **absolute anonymity**. It was to be logged only as an *anonymous community contribution*. The friend who was helping me—she knew the amount, she knew the timing, but she insisted she knew nothing about the payment. I didn't believe her, but she swore she did not have that kind of money, and that the donation had to be divine."

This detail was crucial, the key that unlocked the divine logic for the rest of the congregation—and for Grace. Sarah, however, focused on the spiritual impact.

"We were saved, entirely, by a **stranger's kindness**. A kindness that was executed in **absolute secret**," Sarah affirmed, leaning into the pulpit. "And from that day forward, I knew I had received my sign. God had heard my prayer, and He had answered it through the secret, selfless action of one person who did not want the credit. He chose a **human vessel** for His miracle, and He allowed that vessel to perform the act completely without recognition, so that the faith remained focused on *Him*."

Sarah's voice broke slightly as she recounted the illness that followed days later—the night Grace stayed up with her—the children's panic, and the sudden, complete return to health on Christmas morning.

"I know now that God sends miracles in many forms," Sarah concluded, her eyes finally finding Grace's, a look of profound, shared understanding passing between them. "Sometimes, He uses an illness to force an admission of weakness. Sometimes, He uses a flower shop to gather the hungry. And sometimes, He uses the secret sacrifice of an anonymous stranger to prove that no act of love, however small or hidden, is ever unseen."

The Final Reconciliation

As Sarah stepped down from the pulpit to a wave of heartfelt applause, the sheer weight of her words settled heavily upon Grace. The narrative had not been Sarah's alone; it had been a perfect, chronological recounting of **Grace's private journey** from despair to purpose.

Grace sat motionless, tears streaming silently down her face, not from sadness, but from a dizzying, stunning **clarity**.

She heard Sarah's words, "*absolute anonymity*," and suddenly understood the meaning of the note: ***"Because you gave in secret,***

Heaven saw in full." God hadn't just *seen* her sacrifice; He had **protected** its anonymity, ensuring that Grace could not claim the credit and maintain her illusion of self-reliance. He had allowed the human transaction to become a divine miracle by forcing the human actor to remain hidden.

She realized, with a blinding flash of insight, that the **eight thousand dollars** that had been returned to her was not compensation; it was a **validation**. It was God saying, *"I saw your attempt to honor Tom, and I accept it. Now, go and use that resource to continue the work, and know that you are not doing it alone."*

The years of bitterness, the pain of the unanswered prayer, the shame of her emotional isolation—all of it dissolved. Tom's death had not been the end of God's conversation with her; it had been the **transition**. God had answered her prayer for Tom's survival with a devastating "No," but He had immediately followed it with the gift of **a new life and a new purpose**—a gift wrapped in the cold, desperate need of Sarah and her children.

Grace looked at the children nestled beside her, their faces rapt with the music now starting from the organ. Lily reached out and took Grace's hand, her grip warm and confident. Grace looked at that small, trusting hand, and the final piece of the puzzle fell into place.

She realized she was not just **part of God's plan**; she was the **answer** to Sarah's prayer. She was the **stranger's kindness**—an instrument of grace used exactly as she was: broken, grieving, and deeply human. Her secular act had been His sacred design.

The memory of Tom, once a crushing weight, now felt like a **benediction**. She remembered his booming laugh, his endless enthusiasm, and his simple, profound belief that love was always the answer. Tom was not a victim of silent abandonment; he was the **first sacrifice** in her return to faith, the reason she was open to the desperate human connection that ultimately saved her soul. His love had paved the way for her own return to love.

As the final hymn, "Silent Night," began, the entire congregation rose, their voices joining in the ancient carol. Grace's voice joined them—no longer trembling, no longer defiant, but strong, clear, and filled with a luminous, profound **peace**.

The long, hard journey of bitterness was over. Grace Lawson, the broken widow, had found her way back to the stable, finding not a demanding judge, but a humble, quiet **light** that shone in the cold, desperate darkness, and she knew, with a certainty that settled deep into her very bones, that the true miracle of Christmas was the **love that sees the secret act** and returns the kindness in full. Her heart, healed and overflowing, was finally, completely home.

Chapter 10: God's Perfect Timing

The profound, luminous **peace** that settled over **Grace Lawson** on Christmas Eve was not a static emotion; it was the intense, volatile energy of a heart suddenly and irrevocably surrendered to purpose. The day after the service, she was no longer just the owner of *Bloom & Believe*; she was the custodian of a divine deposit. The **eight thousand dollars**, the concrete proof of Heaven's witness, had sat in her account for a year, a potent but dormant symbol. Now, it was time for that symbol to become **the engine of grace**.

Grace and **Sarah Miller** spent the week between Christmas and the New Year in a whirlwind of focused, joyful creation, fueled by countless cups of coffee and an urgent sense of destiny. They formally established the **Deposit of Trust (DoT)**, registering it with the state as a private, non-profit emergency fund. Pastor Daniel Hayes, his face beaming with quiet pride, agreed to lend his church's name and reputation as the sponsoring organization, providing the necessary infrastructure and accountability.

Grace, the former accountant, was meticulous. She drafted the mission statement, which was anchored on the principle she had learned the hard way: **Perfect Timing**. The DoT would not provide long-term assistance or replace existing social services. It would specialize in intervening in the **critical 48-hour window**—the time between a final eviction notice and the lock change, or between a sudden medical debt and the utility cutoff. It was designed to prevent crisis from spiraling into collapse, recognizing that the difference between ruin and stability was often less than five hundred dollars and two days.

Sarah, the newly appointed coordinator, was the indispensable heart of the operation. She developed the intake protocols, leveraging her deep, personal understanding of desperation to ensure every interaction was handled with **swiftness and dignity**. She knew the language of fear, and she countered it with the language of unwavering, practical empathy.

The seed money—Grace's returned $8,000—was matched by an anonymous donation of $2,000 from the church's reserve fund, and small, weekly offerings from the congregation added modest, recurring growth. By mid-January, the DoT had a working capital of nearly **thirteen thousand dollars**.

The Work of the Covenant

The true test of the DoT began immediately with the onset of the deepest, most punishing phase of the New England winter. The work was intense, quiet, and profoundly effective.

Grace and Sarah moved with the synchronized purpose of seasoned partners. A panicked call from a school principal about a family whose electricity had been cut off? Sarah verified the details within an hour, and Grace was on the phone to the power company, wiring the exact past-due amount. A young mother facing eviction due to an unexpected car repair bill that crippled her rent payment? Sarah negotiated a three-day extension, and Grace covered the gap. They bought heating oil for a freezing elderly couple, ensuring their survival until their next social security check arrived.

Every intervention was a triumphant affirmation of Grace's restored faith, proving that the miracle hadn't been an isolated event, but a **call to continuous obedience**. She saw the relief flood the faces of the people they helped—the sudden, blessed return of hope—and she knew, with absolute certainty, that this was where her life was meant to be lived. She was not a distant benefactor; she was the **instrument of perfect timing**.

Lily and Ben were woven into the tapestry of the work. Lily, now a quiet, serious ten-year-old, helped Sarah organize the receipt files, learning the true cost of human vulnerability. Ben, seven, simply filled the back office with noise and chaos, his presence a constant, cheerful reminder of the childhood terror that had set this entire design in motion. They were Grace's family, and the mission of the DoT was their inheritance.

The Inexorable Draining

However, as the winter deepened into February, Grace, the disciplined accountant, watched the balance sheet with mounting, familiar anxiety. Human crisis, she realized, was infinite. Their resources were not.

The **Deposit of Trust**, though effective, was perpetually being **outpaced by the sheer volume of need**. The initial eight thousand dollars and its subsequent small growth were being drained by one critical intervention after another. Each life they stabilized drew down the account, leaving them running on a rapidly diminishing reserve.

Grace sat alone one frigid afternoon, reviewing the quarterly statements. The balance was dangerously low—barely **fifteen thousand dollars** remaining. It was more than she had before Tom's death, but now she measured the money not against her own personal fear, but against the fear of her entire community.

She realized her fundamental error: she had treated the Deposit of Trust as *her* personal act of penance and obedience, funded by *her* private miracle money. She had kept the source of the fund a closely guarded secret, believing the anonymity honored God. But now, the **work was suffering** for the sake of the secret.

"If we get two more eviction notices in March, we are done," she whispered to the empty room, echoing Sarah's earlier, bleak assessment. "We will have to shut down until summer."

The prospect was devastating. The fund, born of a **secret miracle**, was now facing the very public, very real threat of **financial exhaustion**. Grace realized that for the DoT to truly fulfill its calling, it could not remain Grace Lawson's private redemption; it had to become **Evergreen Valley's Trust**. It needed to move from a whispered secret to a **public, shared covenant**—a realization that demanded Grace finally step out of the shadows and share the impossible truth of the eight thousand dollars.

The fear was back, not the financial fear, but the deep, existential fear of **vulnerability**—the fear of standing exposed before her community. She knew, with a sinking heart, that the time for silence was over. The Deposit of Trust needed a capital injection of faith, and that meant she had to tell them **everything**. The stage was set for a public appeal, but before she could formulate a plan, the true catalyst for that public action arrived with the first thaw of March.

Chapter 11: The Deposit

The profound, luminous **peace** that had settled over **Grace Lawson** during the last holy night of Christmas was not a static emotion; it was a **fuel** for action, a constant, underlying source of energy that propelled her and **Sarah Miller** into the New Year. The calendar turned to January, then February, bringing with it the coldest, most punishing phase of a New England winter. This severe weather tested the nascent **Deposit of Trust (DoT)** fund almost to the breaking point.

The fund, still primarily capitalized by Grace's returned **eight thousand dollars** and small, anonymous weekly contributions from the church congregation, was meticulously managed. Sarah, with a keen understanding of desperation, established protocols that prioritized swiftness and dignity. They bought oil for a freezing elderly couple, covered a sudden emergency room co-pay for a single father, and, most frequently, negotiated with utility companies to prevent power cutoffs that would endanger children. The fund was working beautifully, proving the efficacy of **perfect timing**—the central tenet of Grace's new purpose. They were intervening in the critical 48-hour windows that defined ruin or stability for a family.

However, Grace, the former accountant, watched the balance sheet with mounting concern. The initial deposit, supplemented by small growth and recurring donations, was being outpaced by the sheer volume of need. Every crisis they averted drained the account, leaving them perpetually on the edge of depletion. It was a terrifying reality check: human crisis was infinite, but their initial resources were not. The fund, born of a secret miracle, was facing the very real, very public threat of **financial exhaustion**.

"We are running on hope, Grace," Sarah admitted one bleak afternoon, looking at a stack of applications they could not possibly address without a massive influx of cash. "If we get two more eviction notices in March, we are done. We'll have to shut down until summer."

The prospect felt like a betrayal of the very miracle that had founded the DoT. Grace had been given the **confirmation** that she was seen and supported, but she was now learning that divine support often requires **human partnership** and **shared sacrifice**. She realized her error: she had treated the Deposit of Trust as *her* personal act of penance and obedience, funded by *her* miracle money. To truly fulfill its purpose, it could not be Grace Lawson's fund; it had to become **Evergreen Valley's Trust**. It needed to move from a private, secret miracle to a public, community covenant.

The Looming Crisis

The catalyst for this necessary shift arrived, ironically, with the first tentative melt of the snow in early March. The aging **Evergreen Mill**, the town's largest private employer and a cornerstone of the local economy for seventy years, announced a major, temporary shutdown. Due to a necessary but unanticipated structural upgrade, the mill would cease operations for three months, laying off three hundred employees with only minimal severance pay.

The news hit the town like a financial blizzard. Three hundred families—nearly one-fifth of the town's working population—faced three months with no income. The immediate and overwhelming result was predictable: utility bills would go unpaid, medical debt would accrue, and rent payments would stack up. The DoT, which had struggled to manage two emergency cases a month, would soon face dozens.

Grace and Sarah sat in Daniel Hayes's study, the balance sheet spread out like a battle map showing impossible odds. The fund contained barely **fifteen thousand dollars**. To effectively cushion the mill workers—providing emergency assistance for basic necessities for three months—they calculated they would need a minimum of **two hundred thousand dollars**.

"We can't do this, Grace," Daniel said softly, running a hand over his tired face. "The church can pledge five thousand, but the capital simply isn't here in small donations. We would need a benefactor. A miracle."

Grace looked at the ceiling, then back at the financial statement. "We already have the benefactor, Daniel. We just haven't told the community who it is, or why. We've kept the *miracle* a secret, and now the **work** is suffering for it."

She finally spoke the difficult truth that had been brewing in her heart since the Christmas Eve service. "I have to tell them, Daniel. Not just the story of Sarah's eviction, which we shared, but the story of the **eight thousand dollars**. I have to tell them the fund was born of an impossible, divine intervention, and that it's God's way of saying, 'I am invested in this town.' We have to take the fear away, and the only way to do that is to replace it with the overwhelming, tangible proof of grace."

The plan formed quickly, demanding Grace step completely out of her cherished anonymity and into the spotlight she had spent five years avoiding. They would host a major event, a **Spring Bloom Gala**, to be held in the magnificent, historic ballroom of the old Evergreen Inn. It would not be a humble bake sale; it would be a sophisticated, high-profile fundraising effort aimed at the entire community, appealing to both civic leaders and everyday citizens.

The Preparation and The Pressure

The preparation became Grace's new crusade. She poured all her professional expertise into the event, designing the floral arrangements herself, leveraging her business contacts for silent auction items, and meticulously managing the guest list. She ensured that representatives from the mill, local banks, and small businesses were prominently featured, making the gala an exercise in **shared civic responsibility**.

The challenge wasn't logistical; it was **psychological**. Every choice—from the type of invitations to the placement of the head table—was an external commitment to a public life Grace had never sought. She was now the face of hope, a position she felt profoundly unqualified for, remembering her own recent crisis of doubt. The pressure of preparing her speech was immense. She wasn't just asking for money; she was asking the community to believe in the reality of the invisible, of a God who intervenes with mathematical precision.

"Are you sure you want to reveal the specific details, Grace?" Daniel asked one evening, reviewing her notes. "The part about the returned money is... intensely personal."

"It has to be personal, Daniel," Grace insisted, leaning on her desk, surrounded by stacks of elegant cardstock. "I spent five years believing God's love was conditional, that my pain was a punishment. That note—*'Keep believing'*—was His direct response to my despair. If I want them to invest their money, I have to invest my **vulnerability**. I have to prove that even the most cynical, most broken heart can be redeemed through this work."

Sarah, her support quiet and constant, offered the final piece of encouragement. "You are telling them that God uses the very thing they are afraid of—**sacrifice**—and turns it into **security**. That's a message Evergreen Valley needs more than money right now."

Grace spent hours in her back office, lit only by the low glow of her desk lamp, wrestling with the words. She realized the story wasn't just about Sarah or the eight thousand dollars; it was about the **timing**—God's perfect, meticulous timing. She needed to show that the miracle wasn't the *giving* of the money, but the *protection* of the anonymity, which forced the miracle to become entirely spiritual, leading her back to faith exactly when the community needed a two hundred thousand dollar shield.

The Spring Bloom Gala

The night of the **Spring Bloom Gala** was magnificent. The ballroom, usually staid and formal, was transformed by Grace's artistry into a vibrant spectacle of color and light. Cascading white wisteria and lush green ivy draped the chandeliers, while centerpieces of vibrant peonies and purple irises adorned every table. The air was electric with the hum of hundreds of conversations, the scent of expensive perfume, and the faint, sweet fragrance of the florals.

Grace, wearing a deep sapphire gown that complimented her striking silver hair, circulated through the crowd, greeting civic leaders, local business owners, and many of the mill workers' families they had already helped. Her smile was genuine, fueled by purpose, and her composure was unshakeable. She was no longer just the widow who owned the flower shop; she was the **catalyst of communal hope**.

After dinner, as the hall quieted, Pastor Daniel introduced her. He spoke with warmth and humor about the growth of the fund, the dedicated work of Sarah, and the immediate need raised by the mill shutdown. Then, he ceded the floor to Grace, simply saying, "Now, please, listen to the story of how the Deposit of Trust truly began."

Grace walked to the podium, her heart pounding a frantic rhythm against her ribs. She looked out at the sea of faces—the expectant, the skeptical, the hopeful. She placed her hands firmly on the polished wood and took a deep, steadying breath.

"Thank you," she began, her voice clear and strong. "I stand before you tonight not as a philanthropist, but as a person who was once utterly, completely lost. Five years ago, I lost my husband, Tom. And with him, I lost my faith, my direction, and my sense of safety. I replaced God's providence with my own financial planning and my own ability to control my world."

She started her narrative by telling Sarah's story, painting a vivid, heart-wrenching picture of Ben crying on the cold doorstep, the looming eviction, and Sarah's desperate, quiet prayer. She spoke of the night of the fever, and the small, desperate prayer she whispered for *help*—the ultimate surrender of her own control.

"And then," Grace continued, her voice dropping to a near whisper, drawing the massive room into her confidence, "exactly one year ago, the miracle that founded this fund occurred. You've heard of the stranger's kindness—the anonymous payment of nearly eight thousand dollars that saved Sarah's family. Tonight, I confess that **I was the stranger**."

A quiet shock wave rippled through the room. Grace waited, letting the confession settle.

"I made that payment in secret," she explained, her voice gaining intensity. "I did it to honor Tom, not God. I demanded absolute anonymity because I was terrified of being seen and judged for an act of compassion. I depleted my savings to do it, and the financial fear that followed nearly consumed me."

She then delivered the final, life-changing truth. "The morning after I made that payment, a hand-delivered envelope arrived at my shop. Inside was **the exact eight thousand dollars** I had spent, returned to me in full. And with it, a note that proved my privacy was an illusion, and my broken prayer had been heard."

Grace held up the small, elegant linen note card, the one she now carried with her everywhere. She read the words aloud, her voice ringing with the authority of the redeemed:

"Because you gave in secret, Heaven saw in full. Keep believing."

"The truth is this," Grace concluded, her eyes shining with unshed tears. "That eight thousand dollars was not a prize; it was a **deposit of trust**. It was God's way of ensuring that my fear did not stop my obedience, and it was the proof that no act of love, however small or hidden, is ever uncompensated. He protected my anonymity for one reason: so that the miracle would remain focused on His power, not my charity."

The Shared Covenant

The ballroom erupted, not with applause, but with a collective, reverent **gasp** that transformed quickly into a powerful, sustained standing ovation. People weren't just cheering the story; they were cheering the proof that their own town was host to a genuine, confirmed miracle.

The remainder of the evening was a blur of overwhelming generosity. The local bank CEO, visibly moved, pledged twenty-five thousand dollars on the spot. Small business owners matched the initial pledge. And the mill workers, whose fear had been the impetus for the event, lined up to contribute five, ten, and twenty dollars each—their own small, immediate deposits of trust.

By the time the final tally was calculated, the Deposit of Trust fund had raised **two hundred and fifty thousand dollars**. It was more than enough to weather the three-month mill shutdown, and enough to secure the fund's permanent future as a cornerstone of Evergreen Valley's safety net.

Grace stood by the large windows, watching the headlights of the departing guests carve paths through the damp night. She felt an exhaustion far deeper than the simple fatigue of managing an event; it was the exhaustion of having finally released her deepest, most guarded secret.

Sarah approached her, wrapping an arm around her shoulders. "You were incredible, Grace. You showed them everything."

Grace smiled, looking out at the shimmering streetlights. "I did, didn't I? And now, the miracle is their responsibility, too. I gave secretly once. Now, we must all give openly."

The journey was complete. Grace Lawson had finally found the **perfect timing** of God's plan—a plan that required her to be broken before she could be built anew, and a plan that transformed her private grief into a public covenant of grace. She knew, with certainty, that Tom's love had been the first, painful chapter, but the ongoing story, the true, enduring **blessing**, was the shared trust of her community, secured by the proof of an **unseen witness**.

The secret was out, and the light had never been stronger.

Chapter 12: The Epilogue

The years had passed, gentle but inexorable, carving deep channels of permanence into the landscape of **Grace Lawson's** life and the heart of Evergreen Valley. The **Spring Bloom Gala**—the night Grace revealed her secret miracle and the town rallied to meet the mill crisis—had not been the peak of a short-lived charity drive, but the **foundation** of a communal institution. Five years later, the **Deposit of Trust (DoT)** was a recognized, federally registered non-profit organization with a small but secure endowment, capable of withstanding local financial turbulence.

The headquarters for the DoT remained, appropriately, within the heart of Grace's world: an expertly renovated, climate-controlled wing attached to the rear of *Bloom & Believe*. The flower shop itself had expanded, its profits now deliberately leveraged to cover the non-profit's administrative overhead, ensuring every donation went directly to families in need. The shop smelled perpetually of earth, growth, and the quiet diligence of shared labor.

Sarah Miller was the Executive Director of the DoT, a transformation completed from the timid, debt-stricken mother to a formidable, eloquent advocate for the poor. Her understanding of the families they served was rooted in her own experience, lending her authority a profound, unassailable empathy. She managed a staff of two part-time social workers and a team of dedicated volunteers. She was no longer running on hope; she was running on **certainty**.

Lily and Ben were teenagers now. Lily, fifteen, was thoughtful and academically inclined, often volunteering after school to help Sarah organize the complex case files. She had the quiet, observant disposition of her adopted aunt, Grace, and the gentle resilience of her mother. Ben, twelve, was pure, unrestrained energy, often tasked with maintenance and deliveries, his presence a constant, cheerful reminder of the childhood terror that had set this entire miracle in motion. They were not merely Grace's neighbors; they were her life's core, calling her "Auntie Grace" with an affection that had only deepened with time.

Grace herself was radiant. Her silver hair, now shorter and styled with elegant confidence, framed a face marked not by the ravages of grief, but by the lines of laughter and purpose. She still managed *Bloom & Believe*, overseeing the intricate ballet of floral design and business logistics, but her true purpose was interwoven with the work next door. She served as the DoT's Treasurer and primary fundraiser, traveling to neighboring towns and even distant cities to tell the story—the story of the **eight thousand dollars**, the note, and the perfect timing of God's intervention. She was no longer asking for money; she was selling the undeniable, compelling evidence of **hope in action**.

A Quiet Act of Renewal

It was **Christmas Eve** once more. The Evergreen Mill, having completed its modernization, was now humming with renewed activity, ensuring a stable economy. The deep, punishing cold had been replaced by a light, celebratory frost.

Tonight, the shop was quiet. The flurry of holiday orders had been completed, and the staff—including Lily, who was paid in advance for her efforts—had gone home. Only Grace, Sarah, and Ben remained, involved in their own private tradition.

They stood in the back office, the new wing that housed the DoT's operations, which was now filled with the organized clutter of their ministry. Instead of decorating a magnificent tree for show, they were packing **Care Boxes**. These were not necessities like food or blankets—the DoT handled those throughout the year—but small, intentional packages designed purely for **joy and dignity**. Each box contained high-quality, non-essential items: a small, beautiful book, a gourmet coffee blend, a hand-poured candle, a packet of seeds for spring planting, and a small, anonymous, sealed envelope containing a **fifty-dollar cash gift** to spend entirely on something frivolous.

Ben, gangly and perpetually moving, sealed the last box with a strip of metallic tape. "Thirty-seven boxes," he announced, puffing out his chest. "The most ever. I hope the little kids get the action figures I put in the six boxes."

"They will, sweetie," Sarah assured him, smiling. Her face, perpetually relaxed now, bore the gentle fatigue of a life well-spent in service. "Your Auntie Grace and I will make sure of it when we drop them off tomorrow morning."

Lily, meanwhile, was carefully placing the thirty-seventh envelope into a special file box. Grace noticed the deliberate, quiet concentration in her movements.

"What's the special file for, Lil?" Grace asked, her voice soft.

Lily looked up, a knowing smile touching her lips. "This one's for the **Eighth Deposit**, Auntie Grace. It's the cash we save from the odd jobs the DoT generates. When the box goes out, this money goes back into the endowment. It's the annual gift back to the fund, ensuring the miracle keeps working."

The *Eighth Deposit*. The name, coined by Sarah, referred to the small surplus they generated and annually funneled back into the permanent endowment, symbolizing their acknowledgment of the original, impossible $8,000 return. It was a yearly, intentional act of **faith renewal**, a physical acknowledgment that God remained the silent, primary investor in their venture.

Grace watched her, feeling a warmth spread through her chest that was far deeper than the office heater. Her lessons were not merely learned; they were being **inherited**.

The Weight of Gratitude

Later, after Sarah and the children had left for the night, promising to return early for the Christmas morning deliveries, Grace walked back into the main shop. She moved slowly, trailing her hand over the dark, polished wood of the workbench, the same bench where she had once guarded her misery and meticulously planned her retreat from the world.

The shop was empty, silent, and bathed only in the warm, perpetual glow of the safety lighting. There was no grand Christmas tree this year; the annual tradition was now focused on the people, not the spectacle. But Grace stopped by a small, thriving lemon tree she kept near the large arched window—a difficult, temperamental plant that needed constant care and light, much like a struggling heart.

She pulled up an old wooden stool, the same stool she used to perch on while cutting ribbon, and sat down. She was completely alone, but for the first time in her life, the solitude was **not lonely**. It was sacred.

She closed her eyes and began her own personal, internal pilgrimage, reviewing the five years since that first Christmas Eve. She remembered the **anger** that had coated her soul after Tom's death, thick and protective, like varnish. She recalled the **shame** when she saw Ben's tear-stained face, and the desperate, almost manic **fear** that drove her to write the check that saved them.

She felt the residual, sharp memory of the **fever night**—the fear that she, the competent, rational Grace Lawson, was utterly powerless. She remembered whispering the broken prayer for *help*, followed by the silence that was, in fact, not silence at all, but the quiet, overwhelming presence of **solace**.

And then the **miracle**—the returned money, the elegant note, and the crushing realization that she had been utterly, profoundly seen by the very God she had denounced. She recalled the **terrifying vulnerability** of telling Sarah, of standing before the church congregation, and finally, the **naked courage** of standing before the entire community at the Gala, revealing the secret to save their town.

Every tear shed in those five years, every doubt that had shadowed her path, every frantic fear of failure—it all served now as **proof**. The pain had been real, the grief annihilating, but the Lord had not left her. He had simply allowed her to hit the bottom of her own strength, so that when the rescue came, there was no mistaking the source.

The Final Benediction

Grace opened her eyes. The light from the streetlamp outside cast a long, silver shadow across the floor. She smiled, a deep, genuine expression that settled the last piece of the past into its proper place. The years of raging at the "Why?" of Tom's death had ended. She finally understood that the absence of Tom had created the **space** for her purpose, and his memory was the permanent **engine** of her compassion. He was not gone; he was woven into the fabric of the community's security.

She bowed her head, her posture one of quiet, unreserved **gratitude**. Her voice, once choked by bitterness, now carried the clear, resonant tone of unwavering certainty.

She didn't ask for anything; she only offered thanks. "**You never left me, Lord**," she whispered, her words echoing softly in the vast, silent space of the shop. "**I just couldn't see You.**"

Her prayer was complete. The light of the small lemon tree shone, a beacon of hope and resilience in the deep winter night. Grace felt the warmth of her quiet sanctuary, the enduring love of her new family, and the profound satisfaction of a life no longer focused on protecting a brittle heart, but on expanding a boundless, shared grace.

The long journey from the black veil of grief to the bright light of purpose was finally over. The widow who had sealed herself off from the world had become the **silent, steady anchor** of her community.

She rose from the stool, ready for the dawning of Christmas morning and the joy of delivering light to thirty-seven homes. Her heart was full, light, and irrevocably **home.**

"**And in the stillness of that holy night, Heaven smiled — for another heart had found its way home.**"

Don't miss out!

Visit the website below and you can sign up to receive emails whenever Bianca Vadivellu publishes a new book. There's no charge and no obligation.

https://books2read.com/r/B-A-IIBUD-VERPH

BOOKS 2 READ

Connecting independent readers to independent writers.